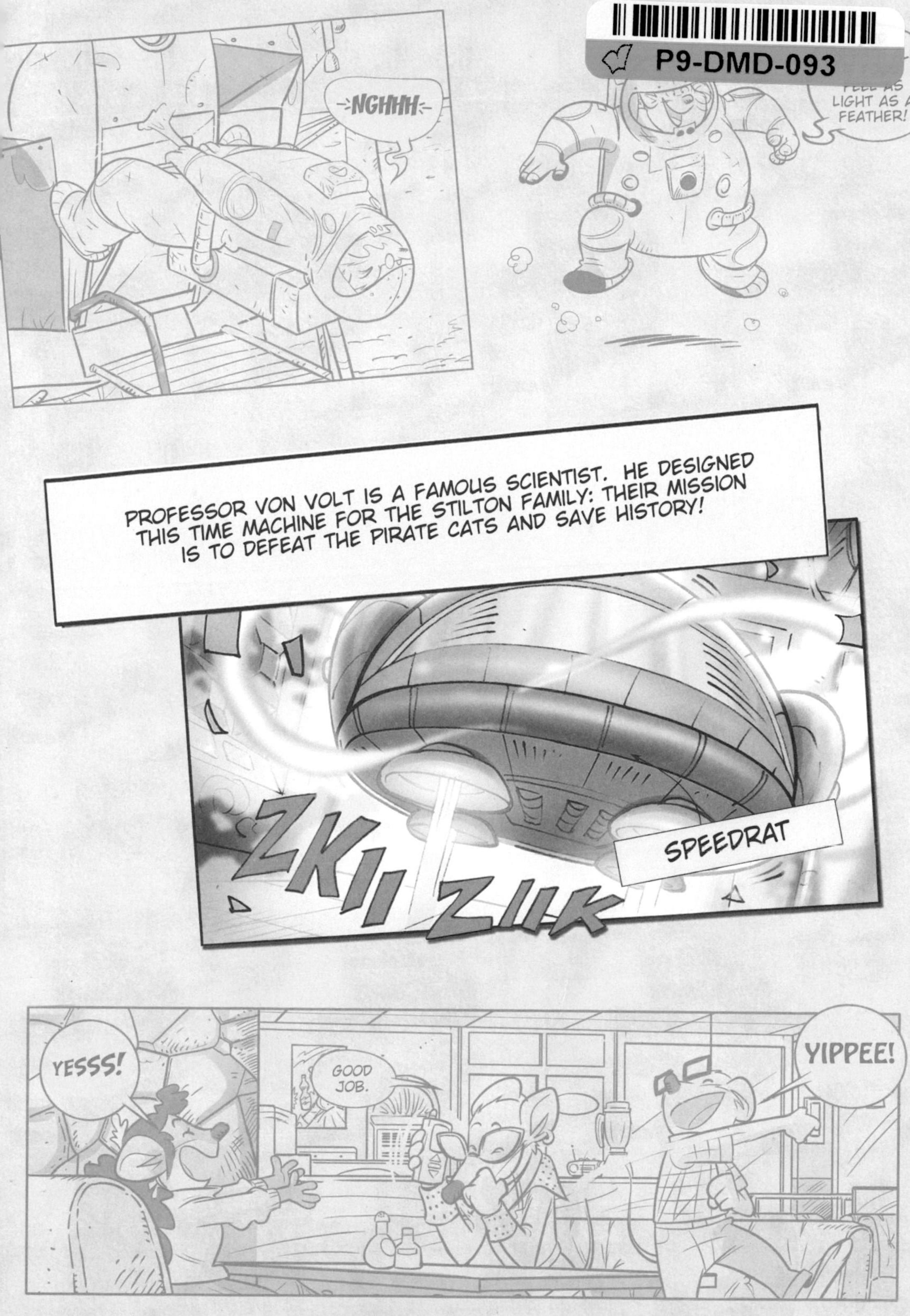
NGHHH
LIGHT AS A FEATHER!
PROFESSOR VON VOLT IS A FAMOUS SCIENTIST. HE DESIGNED THIS TIME MACHINE FOR THE STILTON FAMILY: THEIR MISSION IS TO DEFEAT THE PIRATE CATS AND SAVE HISTORY!
ZKII ZIIK
SPEEDRAT
YESSS!
GOOD JOB.
YIPPEE!

Geronimo Stilton

PAPERCUT**Z**™

Geronimo Stilton & Thea Stilton

GRAPHIC NOVELS AVAILABLE FROM PAPERCUTZ™

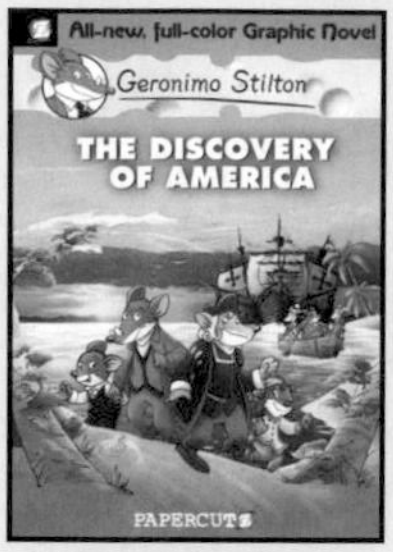
All-new, full-color Graphic Novel
Geronimo Stilton
THE DISCOVERY OF AMERICA
PAPERCUTZ

#1 "The Discovery of America"

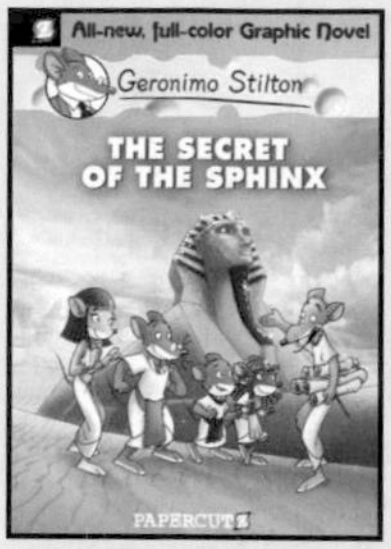
All-new, full-color Graphic Novel
Geronimo Stilton
THE SECRET OF THE SPHINX
PAPERCUTZ

#2 "The Secret of the Sphinx"

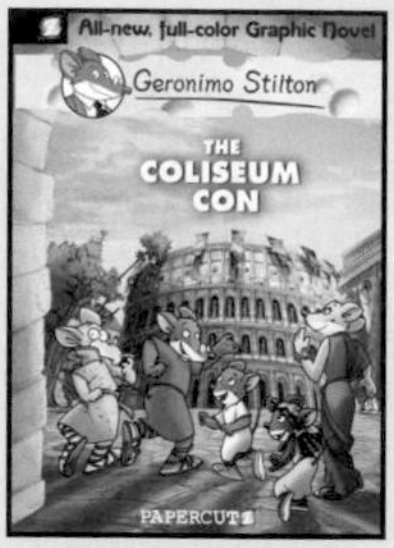
All-new, full-color Graphic Novel
Geronimo Stilton
THE COLISEUM CON
PAPERCUTZ

#3 "The Coliseum Con"

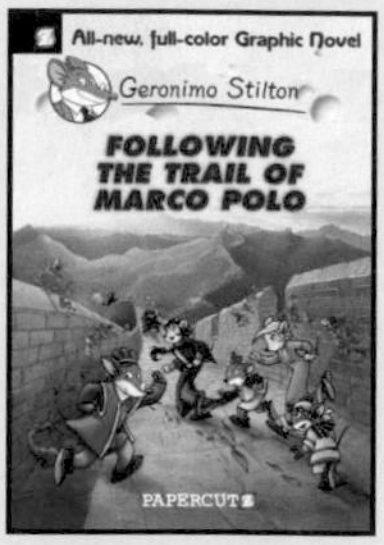
All-new, full-color Graphic Novel
Geronimo Stilton
FOLLOWING THE TRAIL OF MARCO POLO
PAPERCUTZ

#4 "Following the Trail of Marco Polo"

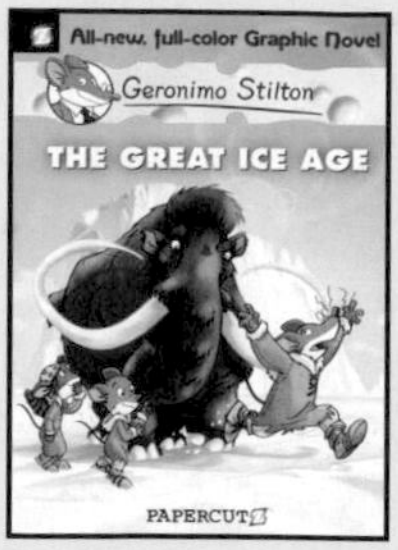
All-new, full-color Graphic Novel
Geronimo Stilton
THE GREAT ICE AGE
PAPERCUTZ

#5 "The Great Ice Age"

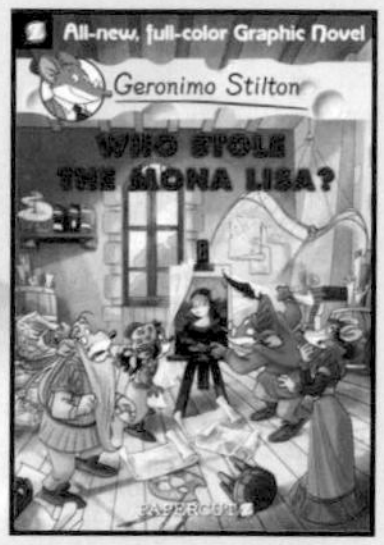
All-new, full-color Graphic Novel
Geronimo Stilton
WHO STOLE THE MONA LISA?

#6 "Who Stole The Mona Lisa?"

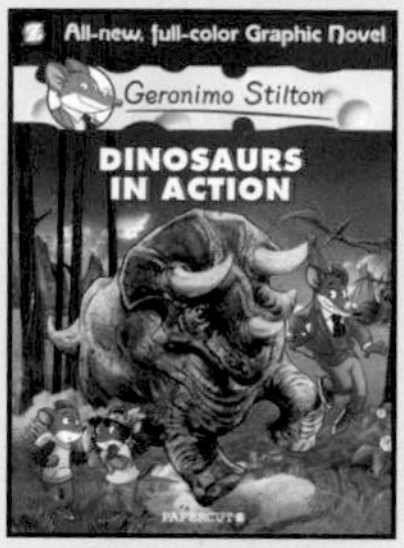
All-new, full-color Graphic Novel
Geronimo Stilton
DINOSAURS IN ACTION

#7 "Dinosaurs in Action"

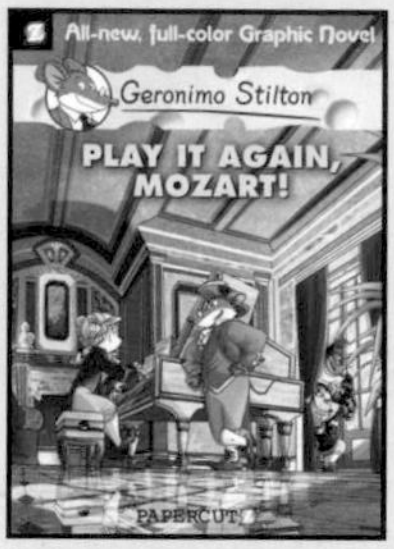
All-new, full-color Graphic Novel
Geronimo Stilton
PLAY IT AGAIN, MOZART!

#8 "Play It Again, Mozart!"

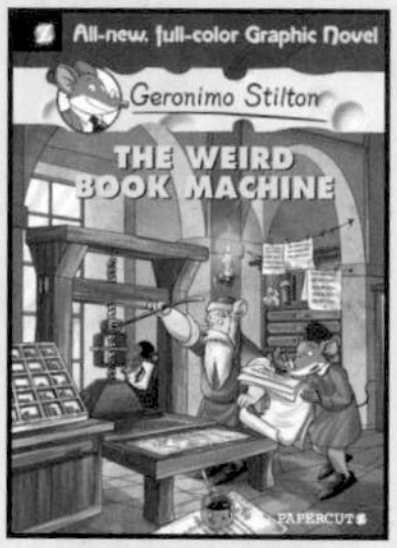
All-new, full-color Graphic Novel
Geronimo Stilton
THE WEIRD BOOK MACHINE

#9 "The Weird Book Machine"

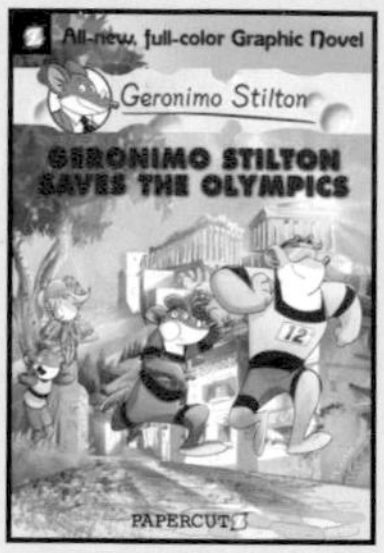
All-new, full-color Graphic Novel
Geronimo Stilton
GERONIMO STILTON SAVES THE OLYMPICS
PAPERCUTZ

#10 "Geronimo Stilton Saves the Olympics"

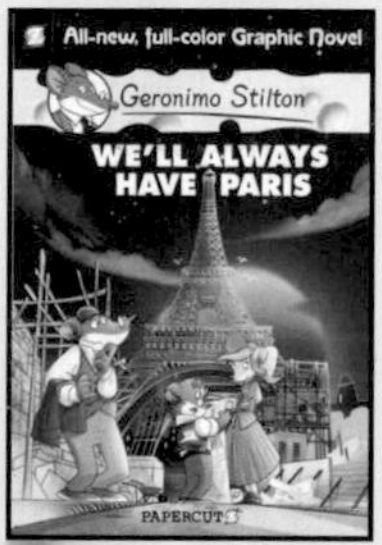
All-new, full-color Graphic Novel
Geronimo Stilton
WE'LL ALWAYS HAVE PARIS
PAPERCUTZ

#11 "We'll Always Have Paris"

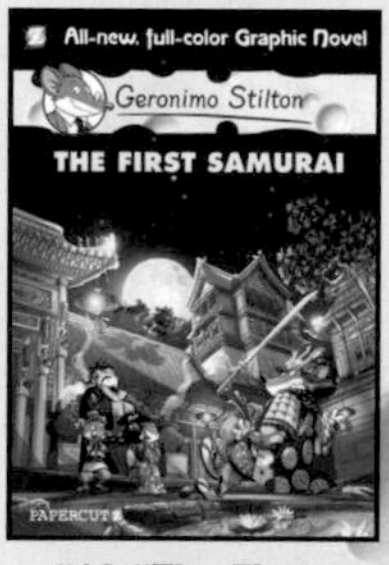
All-new, full-color Graphic Novel
Geronimo Stilton
THE FIRST SAMURAI
PAPERCUTZ

#12 "The First Samurai"

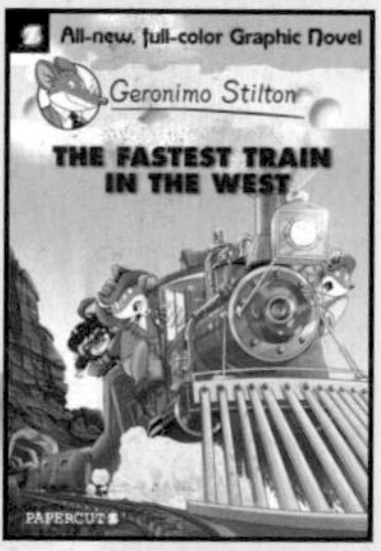
All-new, full-color Graphic Novel
Geronimo Stilton
THE FASTEST TRAIN IN THE WEST
PAPERCUTZ

#13 "The Fastest Train in the West"

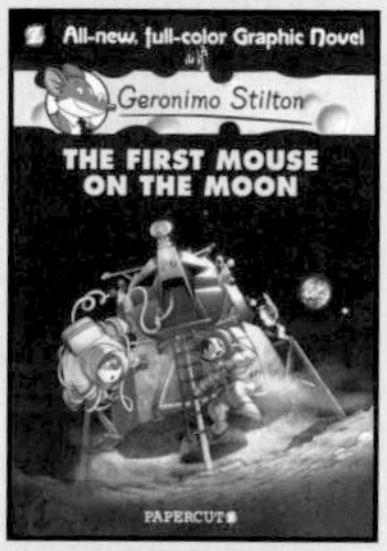
All-new, full-color Graphic Novel
Geronimo Stilton
THE FIRST MOUSE ON THE MOON
PAPERCUTZ

#14 "The First Mouse on the Moon"

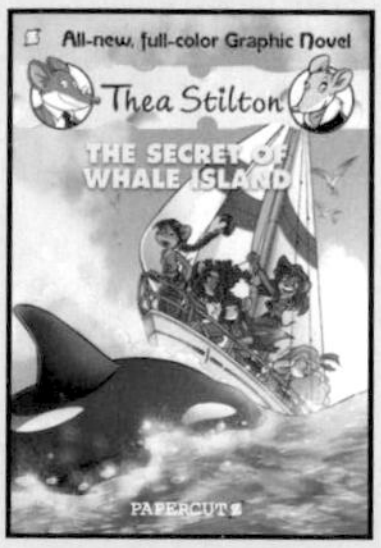
All-new, full-color Graphic Novel
Thea Stilton
THE SECRET OF WHALE ISLAND
PAPERCUTZ

#1 "The Secret of Whale Island"

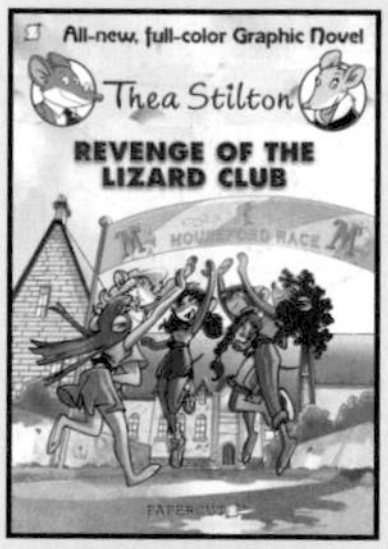
All-new, full-color Graphic Novel
Thea Stilton
REVENGE OF THE LIZARD CLUB

#2 "Revenge of the Lizard Club"

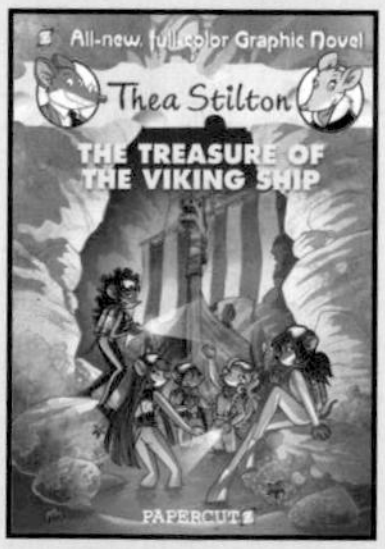
All-new, full-color Graphic Novel
Thea Stilton
THE TREASURE OF THE VIKING SHIP
PAPERCUTZ

#3 "The Treasure of the Viking Ship"

GERONIMO STILTON and THEA STILTON graphic novels are available for $9.99 each only in hardcover. Available from booksellers everywhere. You can also order online from papercutz.com. Or call 1-800-886-1223, Monday through Friday, 9 – 5 EST. MC, Visa, and AmEx accepted. To order by mail, please add $4.00 for postage and handling for first book ordered, $1.00 for each additional book and make check payable to NBM Publishing. Send to: Papercutz, 160 Broadway, Suite 700, East Wing, New York, NY 10038. GERONIMO STILTON and THEA STILTON graphic novels are also available digitally wherever e-books are sold.

papercutz.com

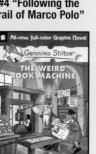

Geronimo Stilton

THE FIRST MOUSE ON THE MOON
By Geronimo Stilton

NEW YORK

THE FIRST MOUSE ON THE MOON
© 2013 BAO Publishing.
Via Leopardi 8-20123
Milan, Italy
Geronimo Stilton names, characters and related indicia are copyright,
trademark and exclusive license of Atlantyca S.p.A.
All rights reserved.
The moral right of the author has been asserted.

Text by Geronimo Stilton
Story by Michele Foschini
Script by Leonardo Favia
Illustrations by Ennio Bufi
Color by Mirka Andolfo
Cover by Ennio Bufi and Mirka Andolfo
Based on an original idea by Elisabetta Dami

© 2014 – for this work in English language by Papercutz.

International Rights
©Atlantyca S.p.A
Via Leopardi 8-20123
Milan, Italy

Original title: "Il primo topo sulla Luna"

www.geronimostilton.com

Nanette McGuinness – Translation
Big Bird Zatryb – Lettering & Production
Beth Scorzato – Production Coordinator
Robyn Chapman – Editor
Michael Petranek – Associate Editor
Jim Salicrup
Editor-in-Chief

ISBN: 978-1-59707-731-6

Printed in China.
May 2014 by WKT Co. LTD.
3/F Phase 1 Leader Industrial Centre
188 Texaco Road, Tsuen Wan, N.T.
Hong Kong

Papercutz books may be purchased for business or promotional use. For information on bulk purchases
please contact Macmillan Corporate and Premium Sales Department at (800) 221-7945 x5442.

Distributed by Macmillan
First Papercutz Printing

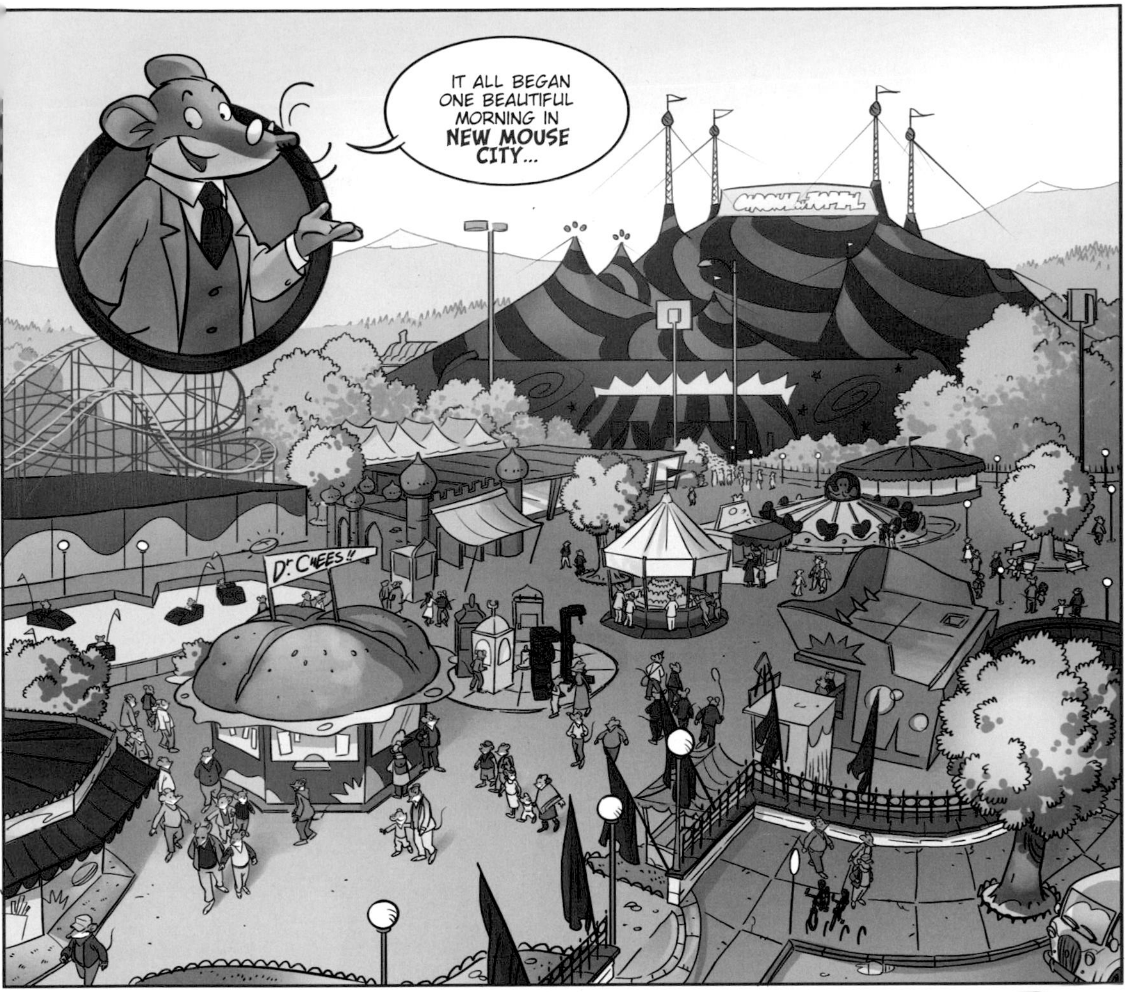
IT ALL BEGAN ONE BEAUTIFUL MORNING IN NEW MOUSE CITY...
Dr. CHEES!!

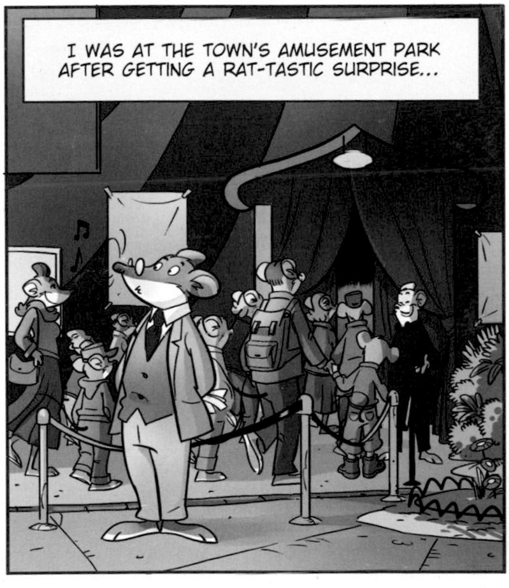
I WAS AT THE TOWN'S AMUSEMENT PARK AFTER GETTING A RAT-TASTIC SURPRISE...

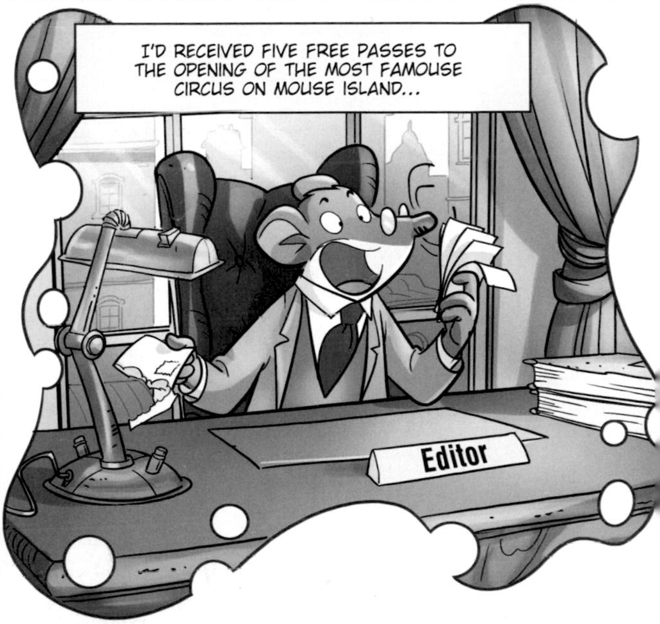
I'D RECEIVED FIVE FREE PASSES TO THE OPENING OF THE MOST FAMOUSE CIRCUS ON MOUSE ISLAND...
Editor

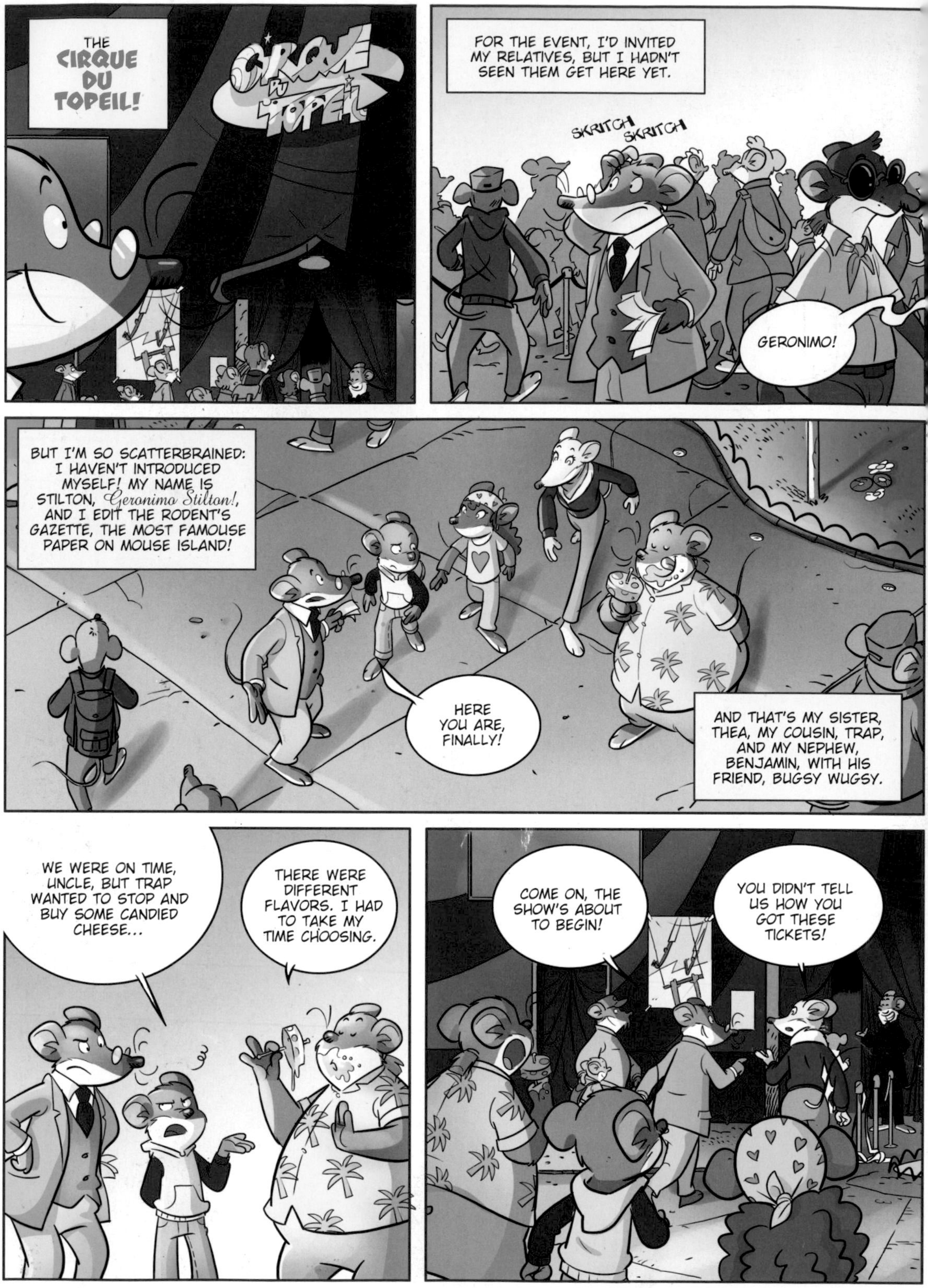
THE CIRQUE DU TOPEIL!
CIRQUE DU TOPEIL
FOR THE EVENT, I'D INVITED MY RELATIVES, BUT I HADN'T SEEN THEM GET HERE YET.
SKRITCH SKRITCH
GERONIMO!
BUT I'M SO SCATTERBRAINED: I HAVEN'T INTRODUCED MYSELF! MY NAME IS STILTON, *Geronimo Stilton!*, AND I EDIT THE RODENT'S GAZETTE, THE MOST FAMOUSE PAPER ON MOUSE ISLAND!
HERE YOU ARE, FINALLY!
AND THAT'S MY SISTER, THEA, MY COUSIN, TRAP, AND MY NEPHEW, BENJAMIN, WITH HIS FRIEND, BUGSY WUGSY.
WE WERE ON TIME, UNCLE, BUT TRAP WANTED TO STOP AND BUY SOME CANDIED CHEESE...
THERE WERE DIFFERENT FLAVORS. I HAD TO TAKE MY TIME CHOOSING.
COME ON, THE SHOW'S ABOUT TO BEGIN!
YOU DIDN'T TELL US HOW YOU GOT THESE TICKETS!

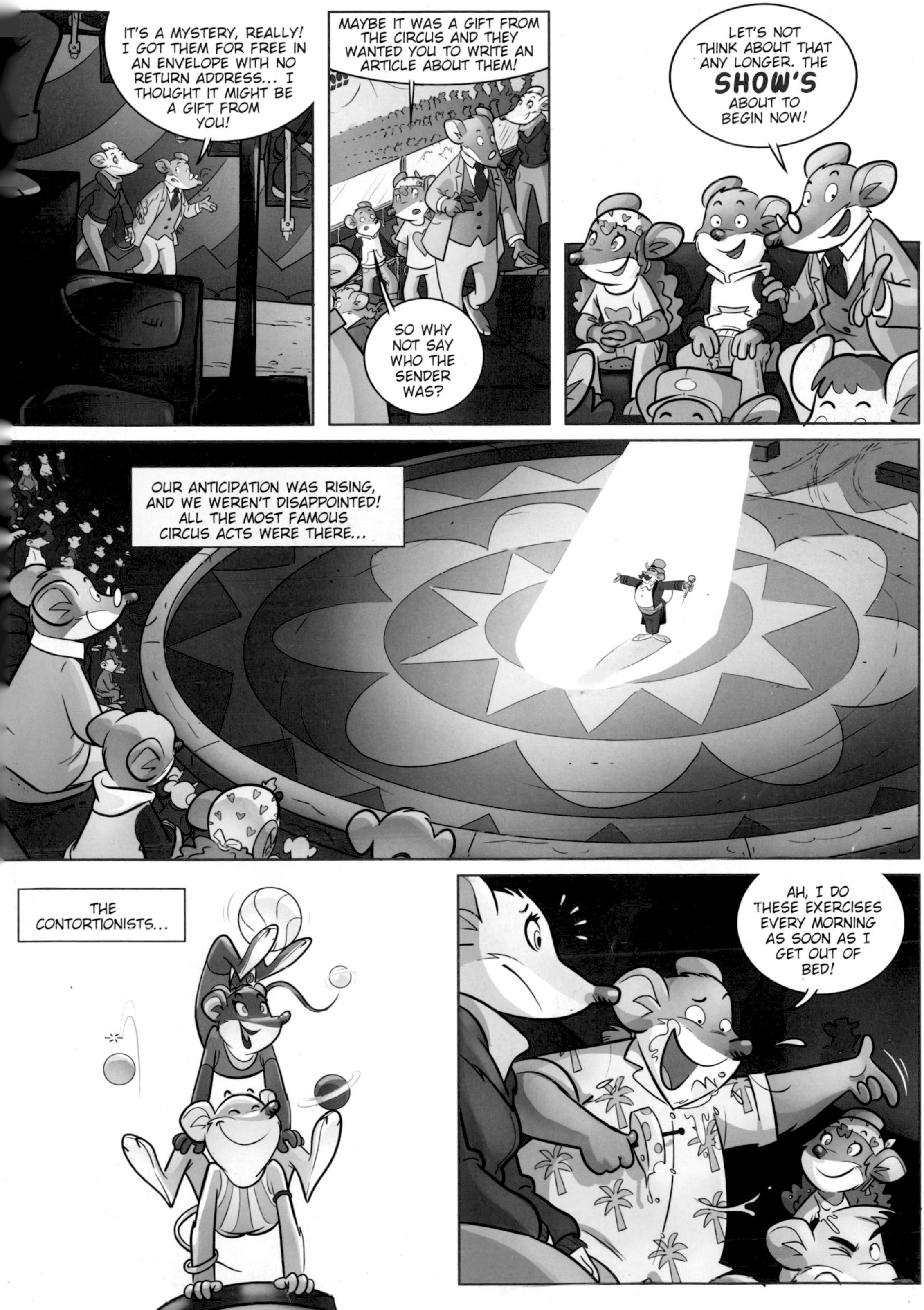
IT'S A MYSTERY, REALLY! I GOT THEM FOR FREE IN AN ENVELOPE WITH NO RETURN ADDRESS... I THOUGHT IT MIGHT BE A GIFT FROM YOU!
MAYBE IT WAS A GIFT FROM THE CIRCUS AND THEY WANTED YOU TO WRITE AN ARTICLE ABOUT THEM!
SO WHY NOT SAY WHO THE SENDER WAS?
LET'S NOT THINK ABOUT THAT ANY LONGER. THE SHOW'S ABOUT TO BEGIN NOW!
OUR ANTICIPATION WAS RISING, AND WE WEREN'T DISAPPOINTED! ALL THE MOST FAMOUS CIRCUS ACTS WERE THERE...
THE CONTORTIONISTS...
AH, I DO THESE EXERCISES EVERY MORNING AS SOON AS I GET OUT OF BED!

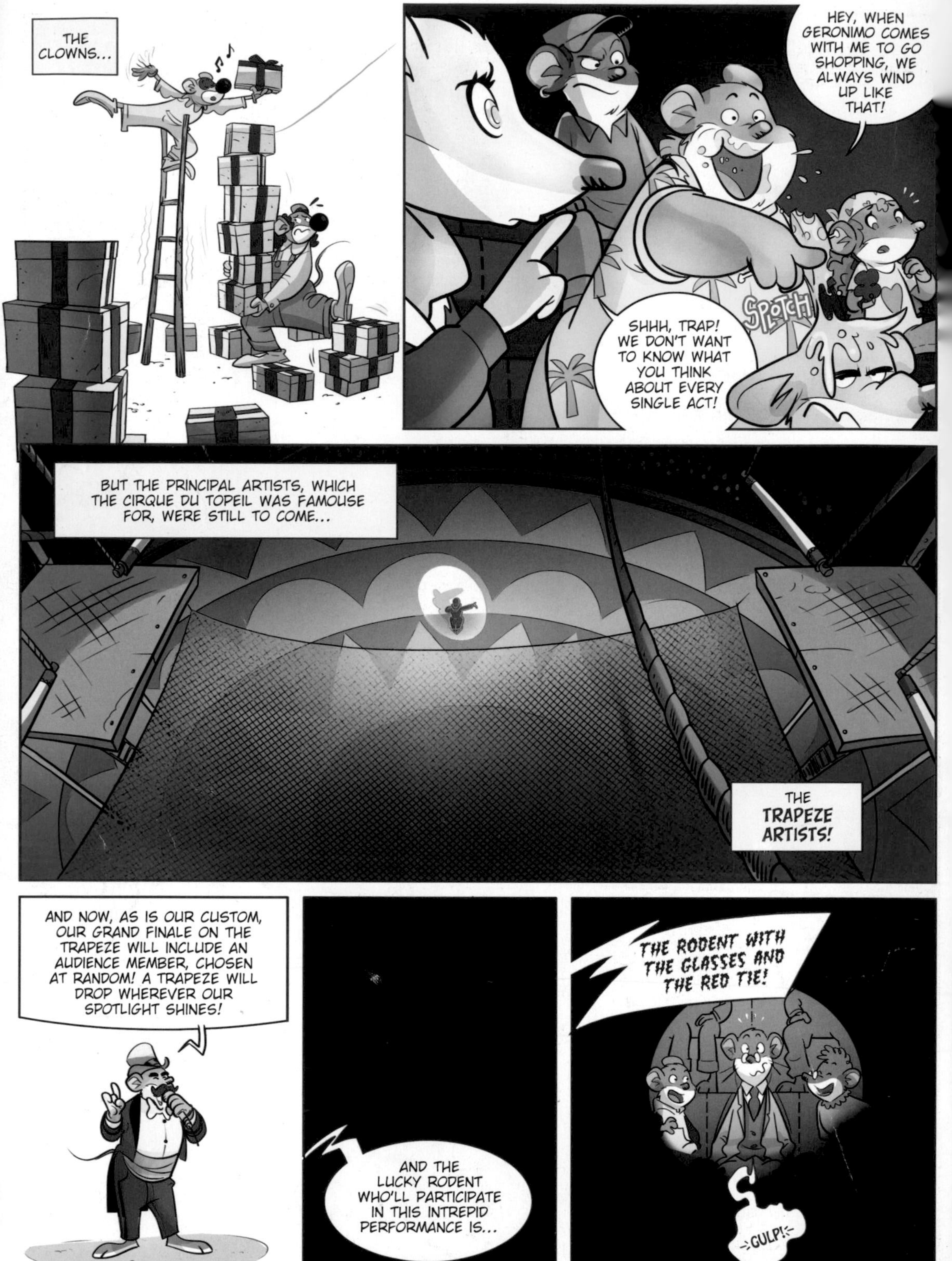

THE CLOWNS...
HEY, WHEN GERONIMO COMES WITH ME TO GO SHOPPING, WE ALWAYS WIND UP LIKE THAT!
SPLOTCH
SHHH, TRAP! WE DON'T WANT TO KNOW WHAT YOU THINK ABOUT EVERY SINGLE ACT!
BUT THE PRINCIPAL ARTISTS, WHICH THE CIRQUE DU TOPEIL WAS FAMOUSE FOR, WERE STILL TO COME...
THE TRAPEZE ARTISTS!
AND NOW, AS IS OUR CUSTOM, OUR GRAND FINALE ON THE TRAPEZE WILL INCLUDE AN AUDIENCE MEMBER, CHOSEN AT RANDOM! A TRAPEZE WILL DROP WHEREVER OUR SPOTLIGHT SHINES!
AND THE LUCKY RODENT WHO'LL PARTICIPATE IN THIS INTREPID PERFORMANCE IS...
THE RODENT WITH THE GLASSES AND THE RED TIE!
GULP!

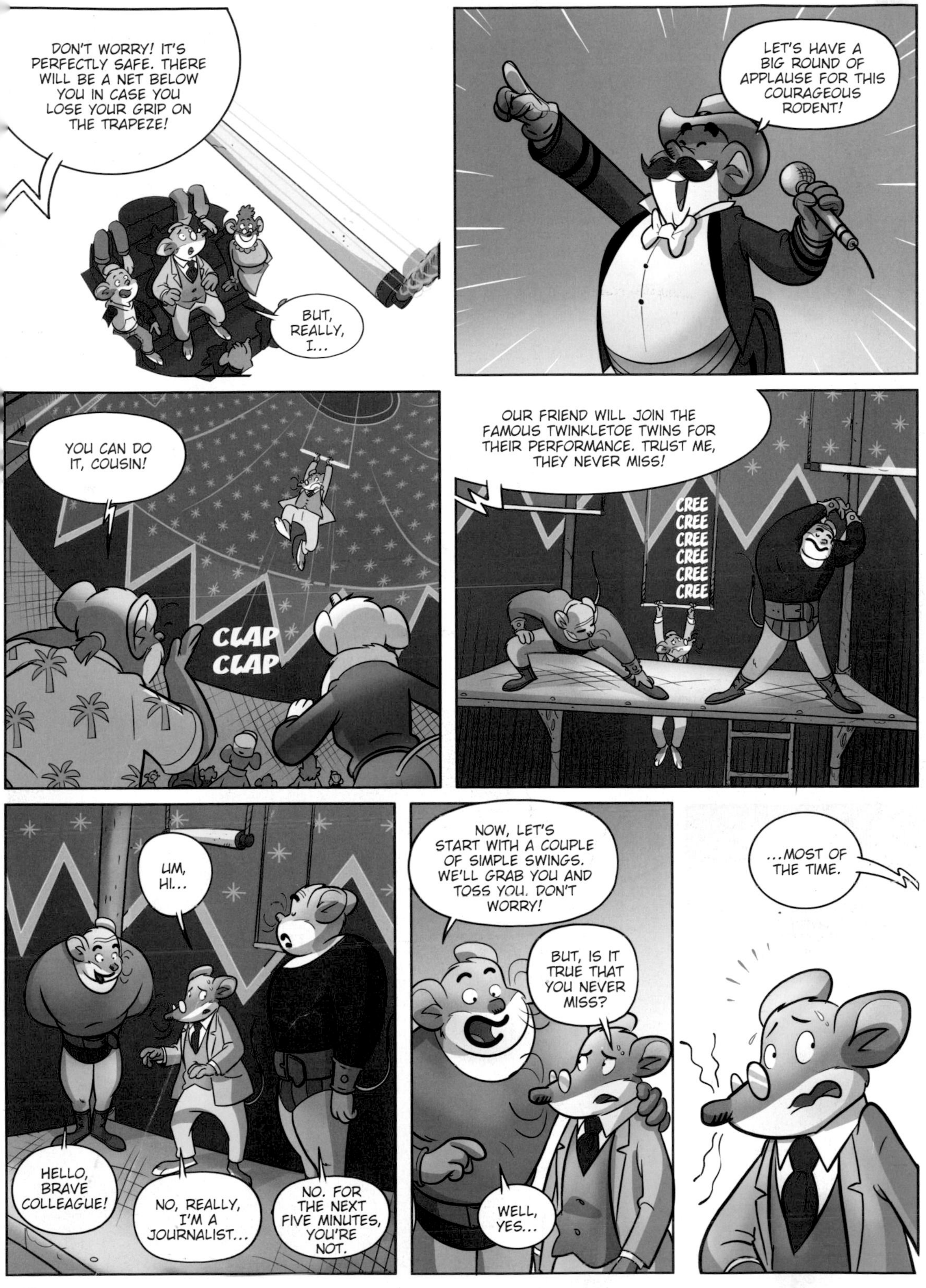
DON'T WORRY! IT'S PERFECTLY SAFE. THERE WILL BE A NET BELOW YOU IN CASE YOU LOSE YOUR GRIP ON THE TRAPEZE!
BUT, REALLY, I...
LET'S HAVE A BIG ROUND OF APPLAUSE FOR THIS COURAGEOUS RODENT!
YOU CAN DO IT, COUSIN!
CLAP CLAP
OUR FRIEND WILL JOIN THE FAMOUS TWINKLETOE TWINS FOR THEIR PERFORMANCE. TRUST ME, THEY NEVER MISS!
CREE CREE CREE CREE CREE CREE
UM, HI...
HELLO, BRAVE COLLEAGUE!
NO, REALLY, I'M A JOURNALIST...
NO. FOR THE NEXT FIVE MINUTES, YOU'RE NOT.
NOW, LET'S START WITH A COUPLE OF SIMPLE SWINGS. WE'LL GRAB YOU AND TOSS YOU. DON'T WORRY!
BUT, IS IT TRUE THAT YOU NEVER MISS?
WELL, YES...
...MOST OF THE TIME.

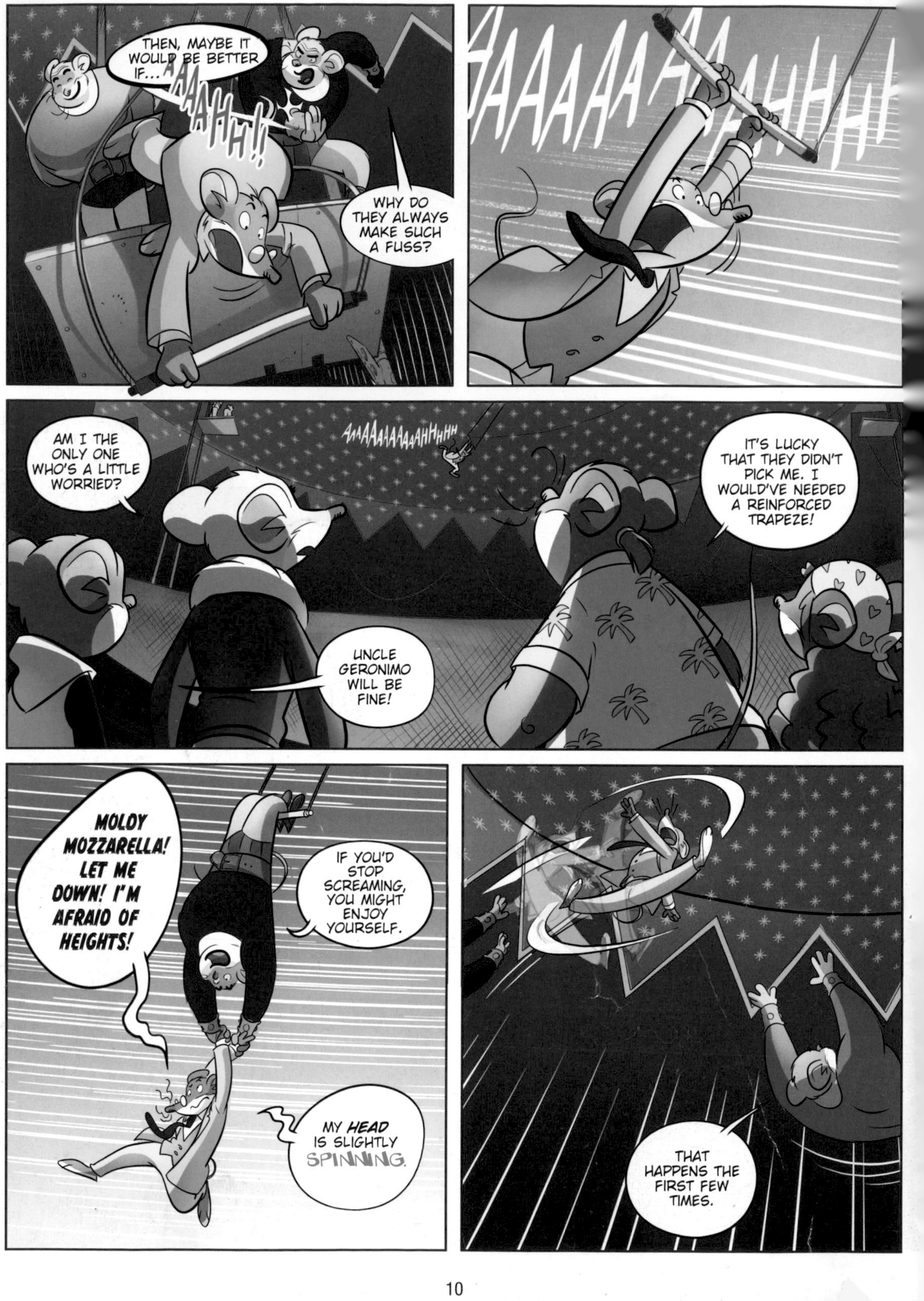
THEN, MAYBE IT WOULD BE BETTER IF...
AAAHH!!
WHY DO THEY ALWAYS MAKE SUCH A FUSS?
AAAAAAAAAAHHHHH
AM I THE ONLY ONE WHO'S A LITTLE WORRIED?
AAAAAAAAAAAHHHH
IT'S LUCKY THAT THEY DIDN'T PICK ME. I WOULD'VE NEEDED A REINFORCED TRAPEZE!
UNCLE GERONIMO WILL BE FINE!
MOLDY MOZZARELLA! LET ME DOWN! I'M AFRAID OF HEIGHTS!
IF YOU'D STOP SCREAMING, YOU MIGHT ENJOY YOURSELF.
MY HEAD IS SLIGHTLY SPINNING.
THAT HAPPENS THE FIRST FEW TIMES.

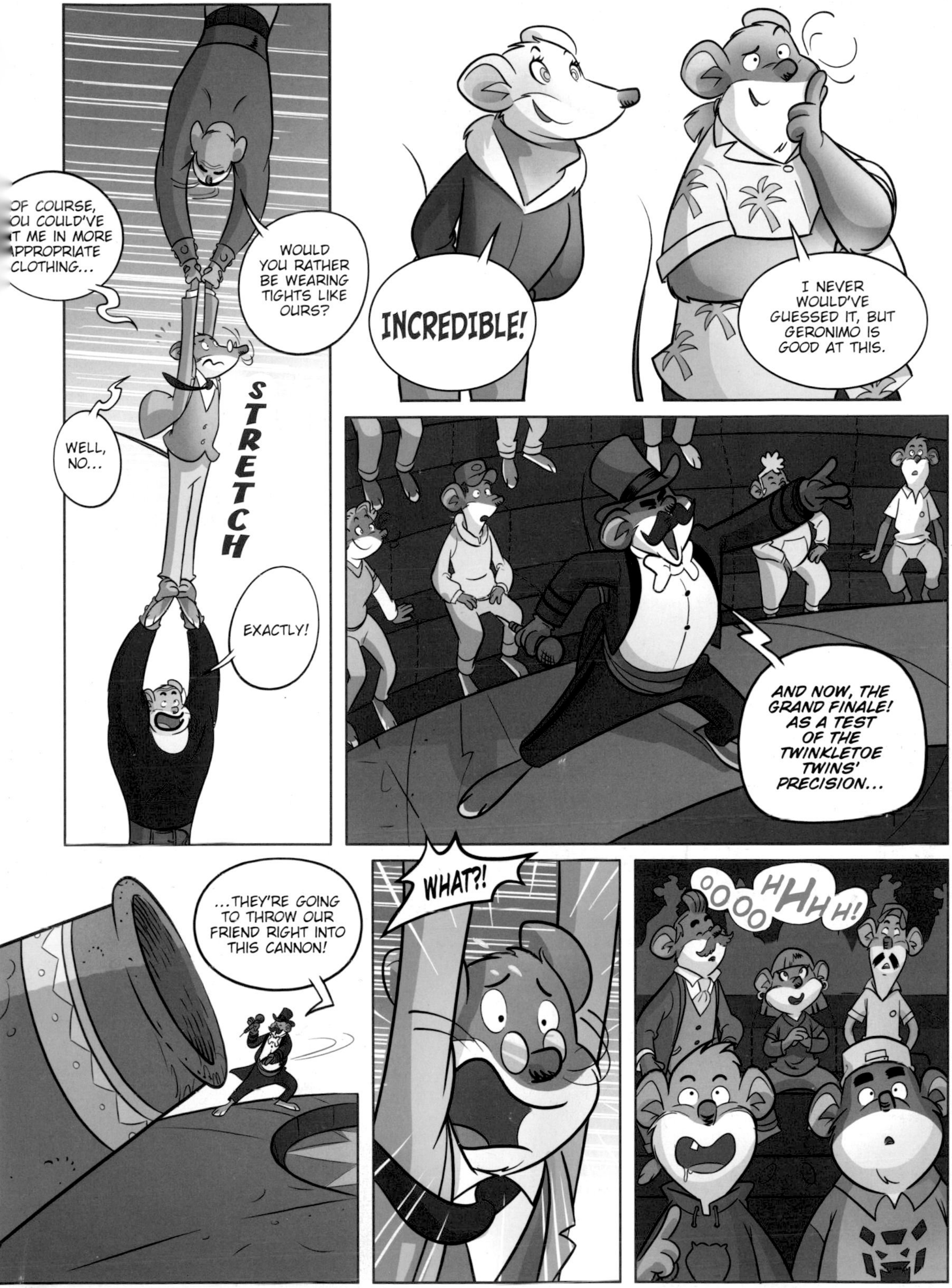

OF COURSE, YOU COULD'VE PUT ME IN MORE APPROPRIATE CLOTHING...
WOULD YOU RATHER BE WEARING TIGHTS LIKE OURS?
WELL, NO...
STRETCH
EXACTLY!
INCREDIBLE!
I NEVER WOULD'VE GUESSED IT, BUT GERONIMO IS GOOD AT THIS.
AND NOW, THE GRAND FINALE! AS A TEST OF THE TWINKLETOE TWINS' PRECISION...
...THEY'RE GOING TO THROW OUR FRIEND RIGHT INTO THIS CANNON!
WHAT?!
OOOOHHHH!

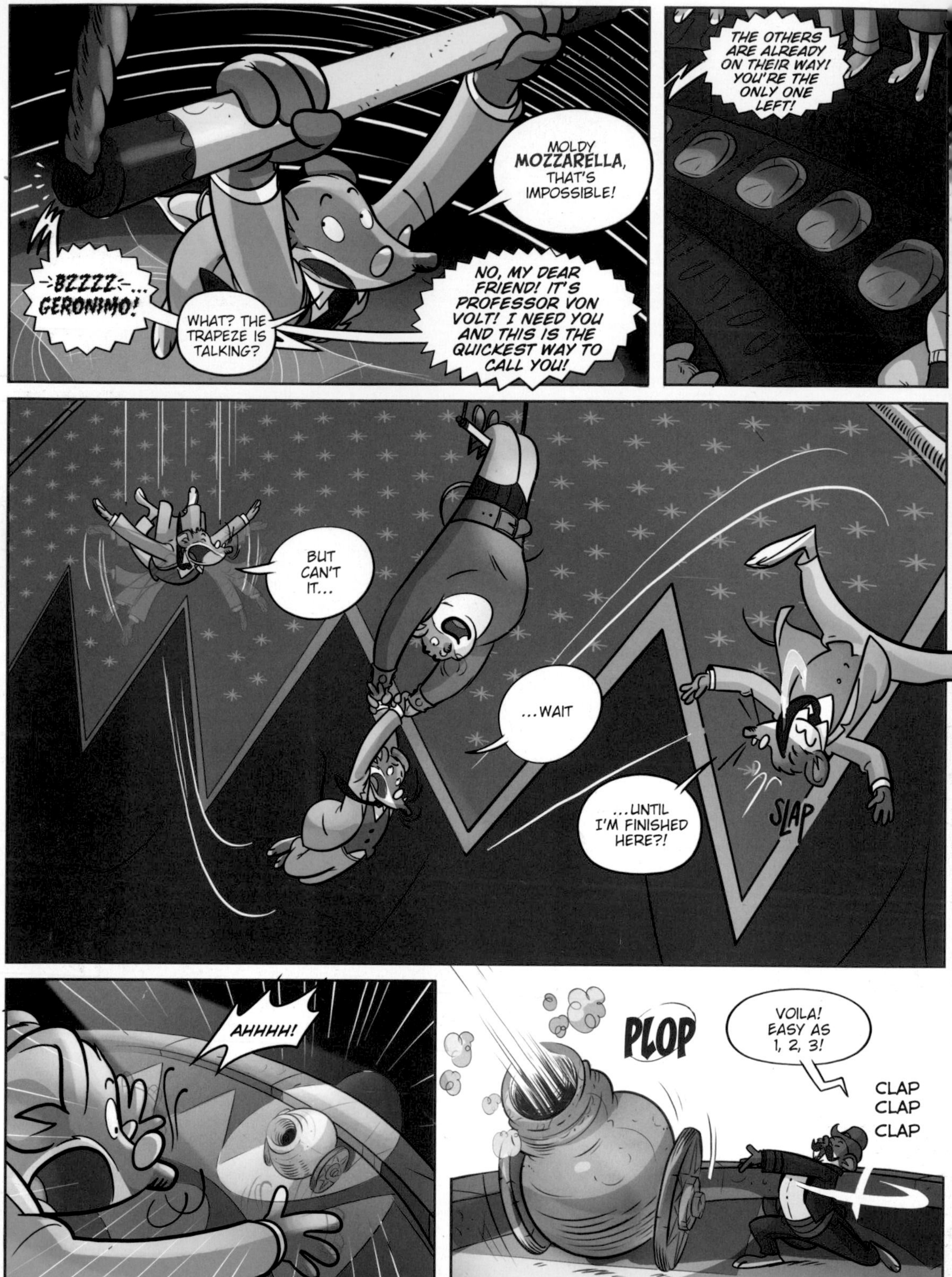
MOLDY MOZZARELLA, THAT'S IMPOSSIBLE!
BZZZZ... GERONIMO!
WHAT? THE TRAPEZE IS TALKING?
NO, MY DEAR FRIEND! IT'S PROFESSOR VON VOLT! I NEED YOU AND THIS IS THE QUICKEST WAY TO CALL YOU!
THE OTHERS ARE ALREADY ON THEIR WAY! YOU'RE THE ONLY ONE LEFT!
BUT CAN'T IT...
...WAIT
...UNTIL I'M FINISHED HERE?!
SLAP
AHHHH!
PLOP
VOILA! EASY AS 1, 2, 3!
CLAP
CLAP
CLAP

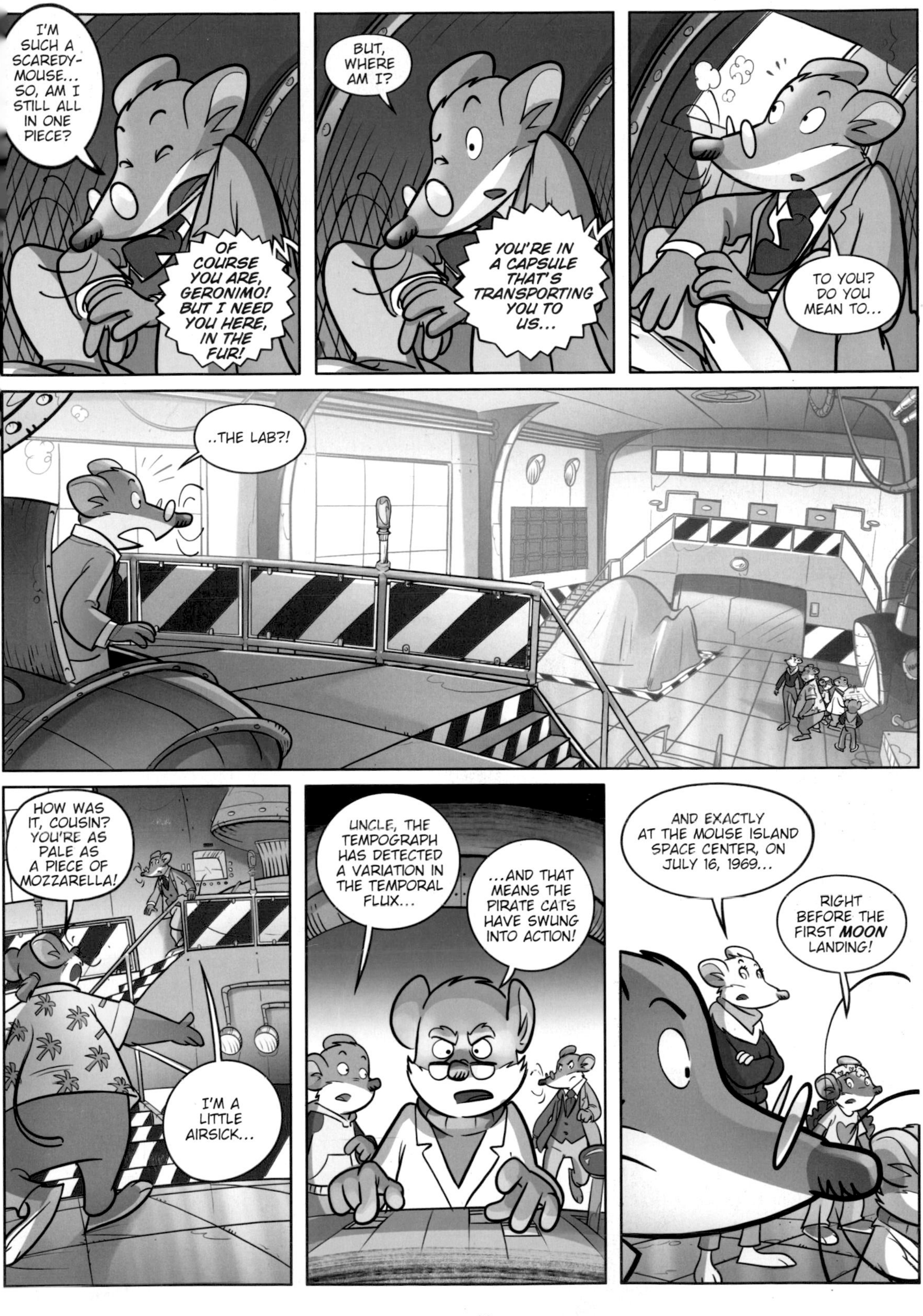
I'M SUCH A SCAREDY-MOUSE... SO, AM I STILL ALL IN ONE PIECE?
OF COURSE YOU ARE, GERONIMO! BUT I NEED YOU HERE, IN THE FUR!
BUT, WHERE AM I?
YOU'RE IN A CAPSULE THAT'S TRANSPORTING YOU TO US...
TO YOU? DO YOU MEAN TO...
..THE LAB?!
HOW WAS IT, COUSIN? YOU'RE AS PALE AS A PIECE OF MOZZARELLA!
I'M A LITTLE AIRSICK...
UNCLE, THE TEMPOGRAPH HAS DETECTED A VARIATION IN THE TEMPORAL FLUX...
...AND THAT MEANS THE PIRATE CATS HAVE SWUNG INTO ACTION!
AND EXACTLY AT THE MOUSE ISLAND SPACE CENTER, ON JULY 16, 1969...
RIGHT BEFORE THE FIRST MOON LANDING!

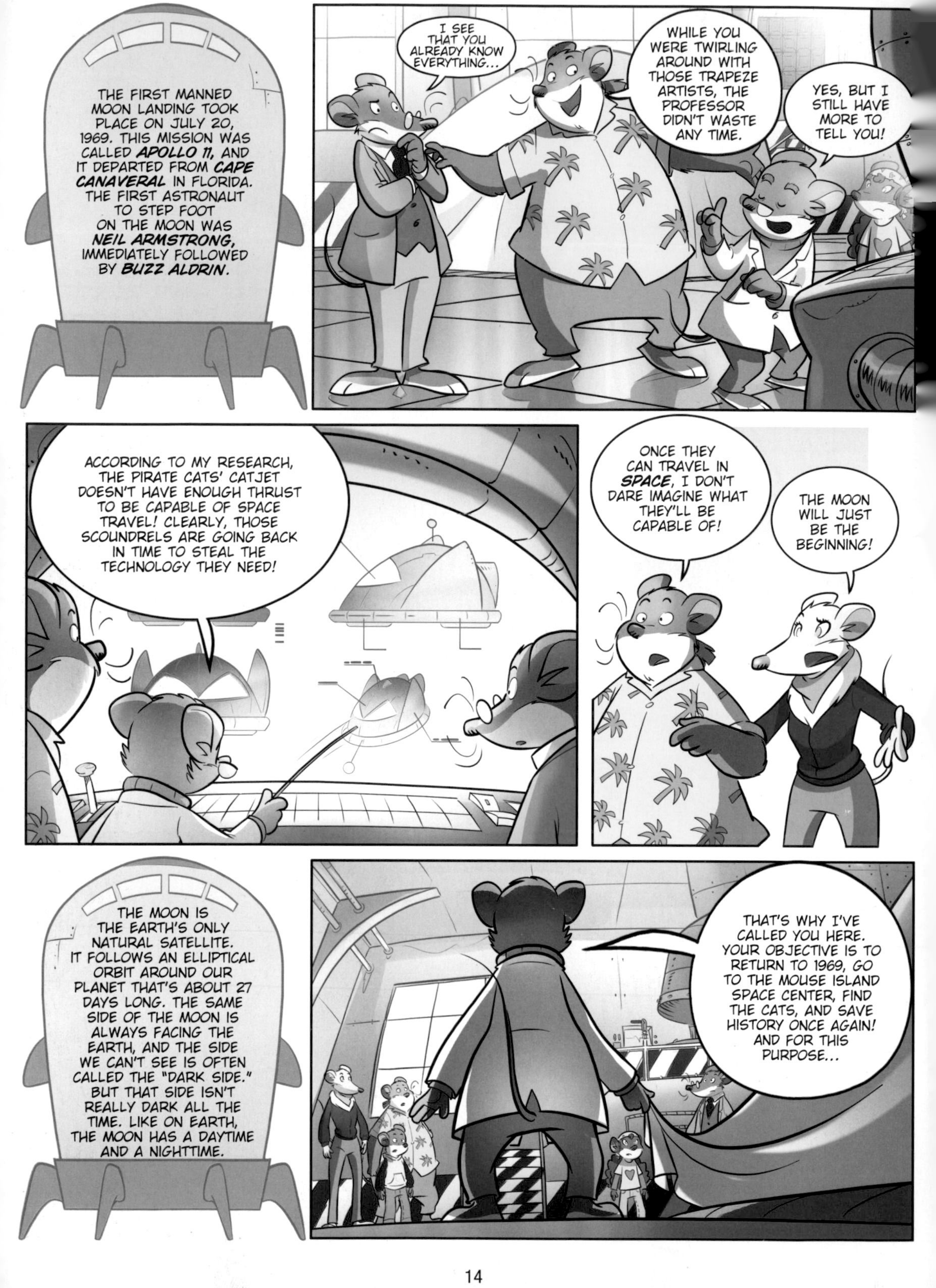
THE FIRST MANNED MOON LANDING TOOK PLACE ON JULY 20, 1969. THIS MISSION WAS CALLED ***APOLLO 11,*** AND IT DEPARTED FROM ***CAPE CANAVERAL*** IN FLORIDA. THE FIRST ASTRONAUT TO STEP FOOT ON THE MOON WAS ***NEIL ARMSTRONG,*** IMMEDIATELY FOLLOWED BY ***BUZZ ALDRIN***.
I SEE THAT YOU ALREADY KNOW EVERYTHING...
WHILE YOU WERE TWIRLING AROUND WITH THOSE TRAPEZE ARTISTS, THE PROFESSOR DIDN'T WASTE ANY TIME.
YES, BUT I STILL HAVE MORE TO TELL YOU!
ACCORDING TO MY RESEARCH, THE PIRATE CATS' CATJET DOESN'T HAVE ENOUGH THRUST TO BE CAPABLE OF SPACE TRAVEL! CLEARLY, THOSE SCOUNDRELS ARE GOING BACK IN TIME TO STEAL THE TECHNOLOGY THEY NEED!
ONCE THEY CAN TRAVEL IN ***SPACE***, I DON'T DARE IMAGINE WHAT THEY'LL BE CAPABLE OF!
THE MOON WILL JUST BE THE BEGINNING!
THE MOON IS THE EARTH'S ONLY NATURAL SATELLITE. IT FOLLOWS AN ELLIPTICAL ORBIT AROUND OUR PLANET THAT'S ABOUT 27 DAYS LONG. THE SAME SIDE OF THE MOON IS ALWAYS FACING THE EARTH, AND THE SIDE WE CAN'T SEE IS OFTEN CALLED THE "DARK SIDE." BUT THAT SIDE ISN'T REALLY DARK ALL THE TIME. LIKE ON EARTH, THE MOON HAS A DAYTIME AND A NIGHTTIME.
THAT'S WHY I'VE CALLED YOU HERE. YOUR OBJECTIVE IS TO RETURN TO 1969, GO TO THE MOUSE ISLAND SPACE CENTER, FIND THE CATS, AND SAVE HISTORY ONCE AGAIN! AND FOR THIS PURPOSE...

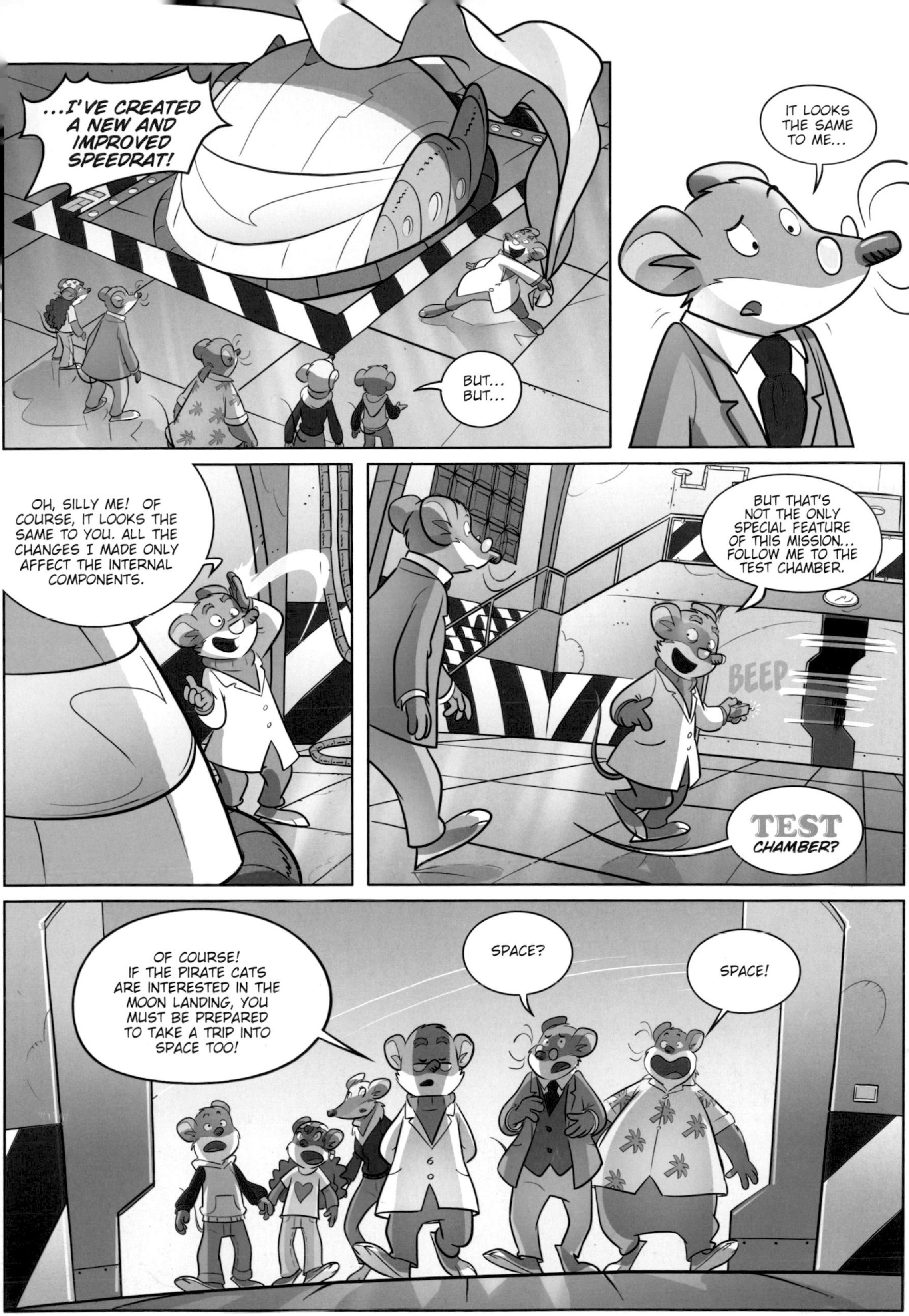
...I'VE CREATED A NEW AND IMPROVED SPEEDRAT!
BUT... BUT...
IT LOOKS THE SAME TO ME...
OH, SILLY ME! OF COURSE, IT LOOKS THE SAME TO YOU. ALL THE CHANGES I MADE ONLY AFFECT THE INTERNAL COMPONENTS.
BUT THAT'S NOT THE ONLY SPECIAL FEATURE OF THIS MISSION... FOLLOW ME TO THE TEST CHAMBER.
BEEP
TEST CHAMBER?
OF COURSE! IF THE PIRATE CATS ARE INTERESTED IN THE MOON LANDING, YOU MUST BE PREPARED TO TAKE A TRIP INTO SPACE TOO!
SPACE?
SPACE!

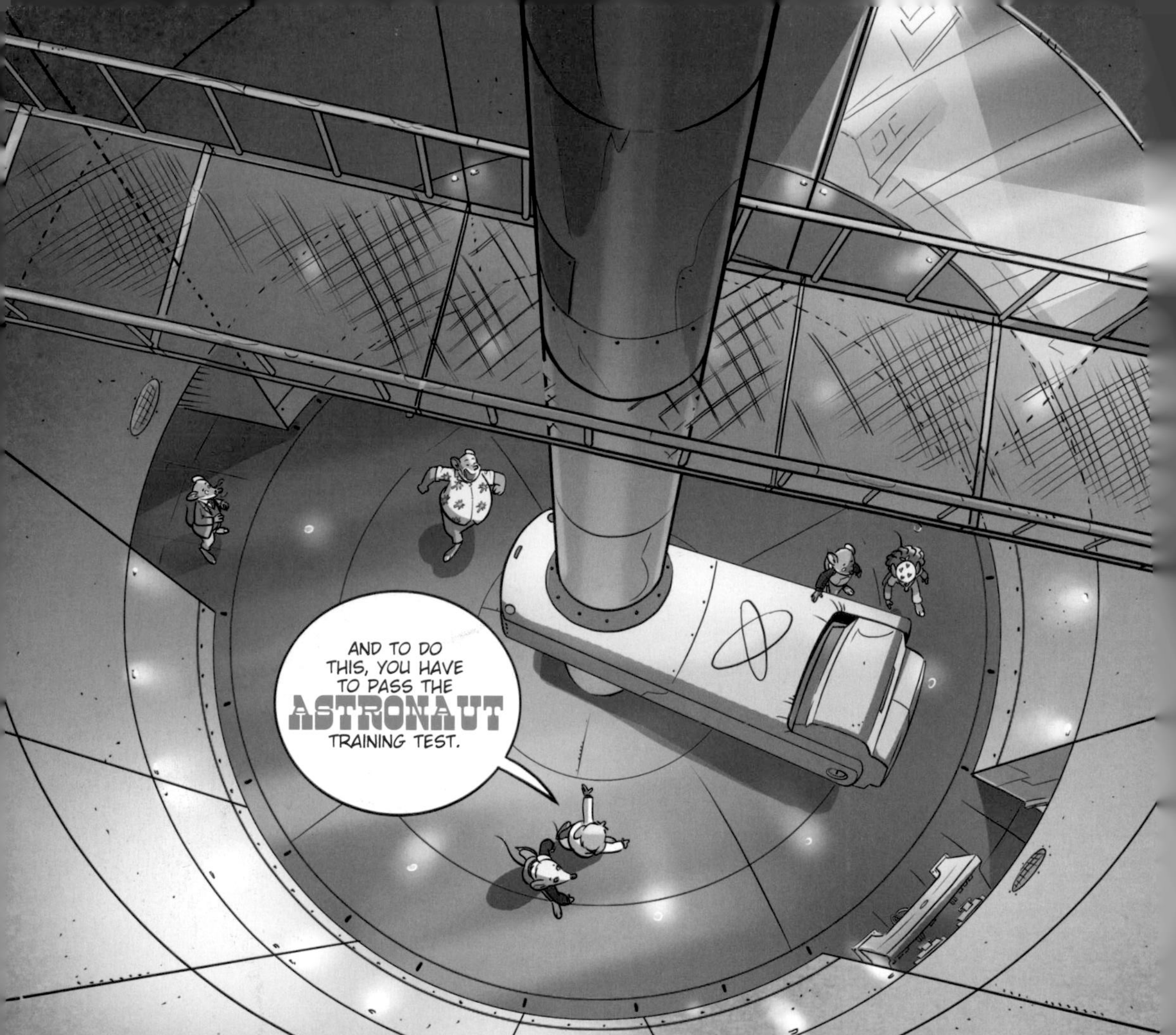
AND TO DO THIS, YOU HAVE TO PASS THE ASTRONAUT TRAINING TEST.

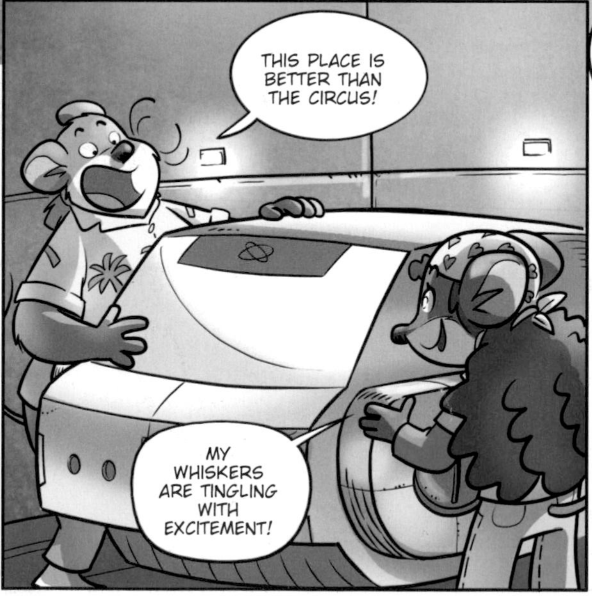
THIS PLACE IS BETTER THAN THE CIRCUS!
MY WHISKERS ARE TINGLING WITH EXCITEMENT!

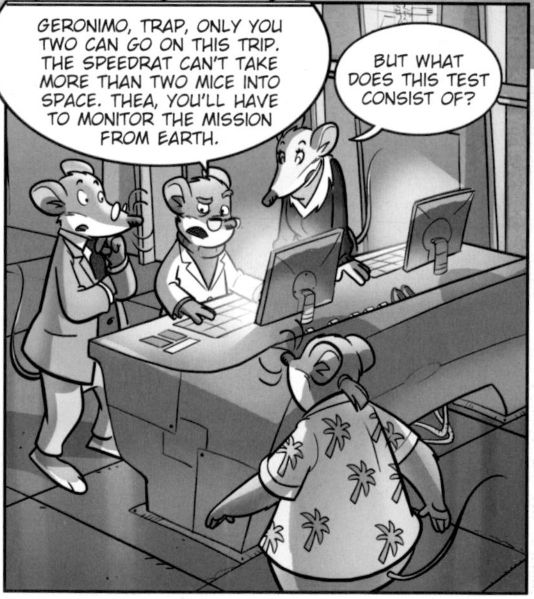
GERONIMO, TRAP, ONLY YOU TWO CAN GO ON THIS TRIP. THE SPEEDRAT CAN'T TAKE MORE THAN TWO MICE INTO SPACE. THEA, YOU'LL HAVE TO MONITOR THE MISSION FROM EARTH.
BUT WHAT DOES THIS TEST CONSIST OF?

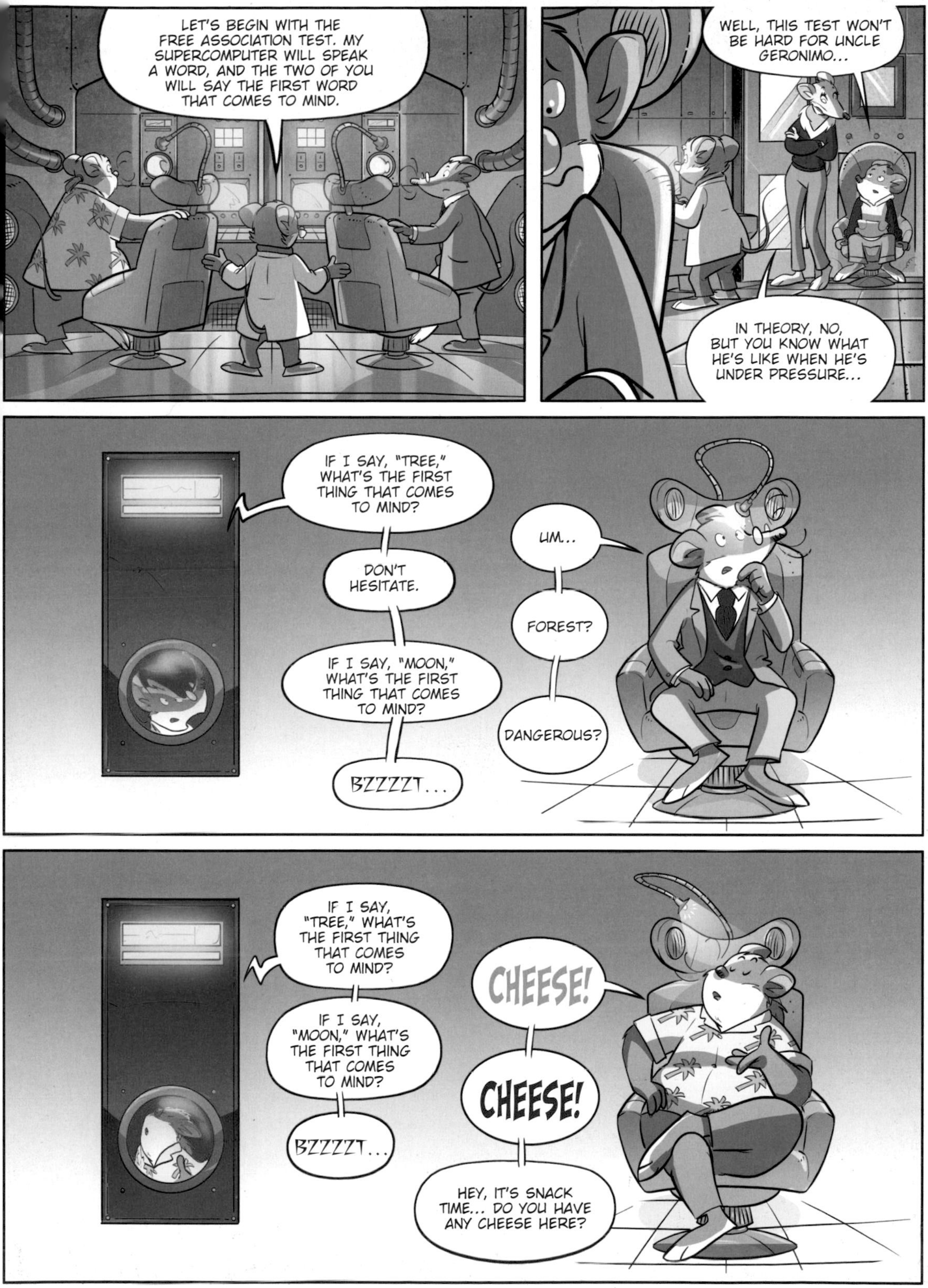

LET'S BEGIN WITH THE FREE ASSOCIATION TEST. MY SUPERCOMPUTER WILL SPEAK A WORD, AND THE TWO OF YOU WILL SAY THE FIRST WORD THAT COMES TO MIND.
WELL, THIS TEST WON'T BE HARD FOR UNCLE GERONIMO...
IN THEORY, NO, BUT YOU KNOW WHAT HE'S LIKE WHEN HE'S UNDER PRESSURE...
IF I SAY, "TREE," WHAT'S THE FIRST THING THAT COMES TO MIND?
DON'T HESITATE.
IF I SAY, "MOON," WHAT'S THE FIRST THING THAT COMES TO MIND?
BZZZZT...
UM...
FOREST?
DANGEROUS?
IF I SAY, "TREE," WHAT'S THE FIRST THING THAT COMES TO MIND?
IF I SAY, "MOON," WHAT'S THE FIRST THING THAT COMES TO MIND?
BZZZZT...
CHEESE!
CHEESE!
HEY, IT'S SNACK TIME... DO YOU HAVE ANY CHEESE HERE?

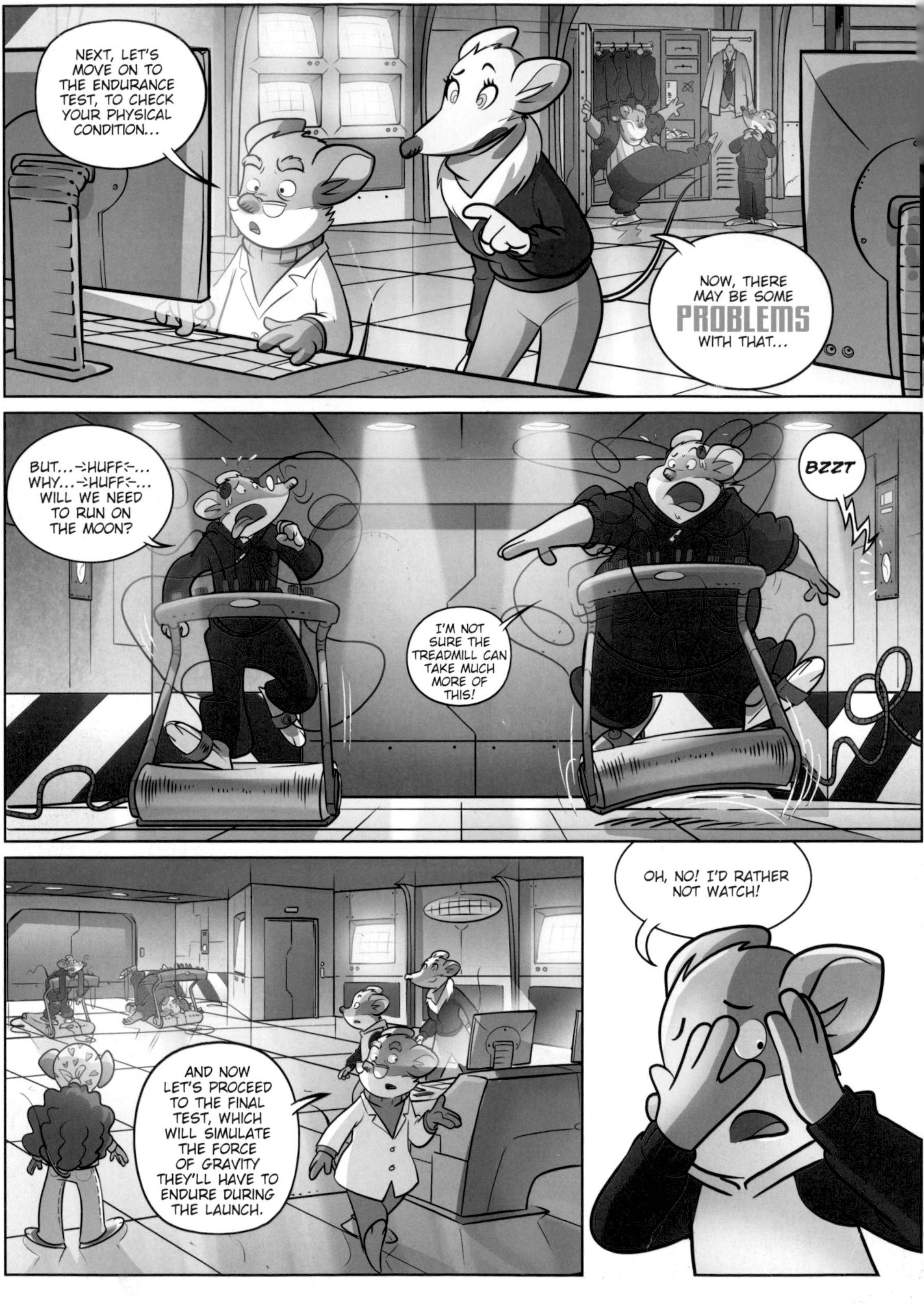

NEXT, LET'S MOVE ON TO THE ENDURANCE TEST, TO CHECK YOUR PHYSICAL CONDITION...
NOW, THERE MAY BE SOME PROBLEMS WITH THAT...
BUT... ⇒HUFF⇐... WHY... ⇒HUFF⇐... WILL WE NEED TO RUN ON THE MOON?
I'M NOT SURE THE TREADMILL CAN TAKE MUCH MORE OF THIS!
BZZT
AND NOW LET'S PROCEED TO THE FINAL TEST, WHICH WILL SIMULATE THE FORCE OF GRAVITY THEY'LL HAVE TO ENDURE DURING THE LAUNCH.
OH, NO! I'D RATHER NOT WATCH!

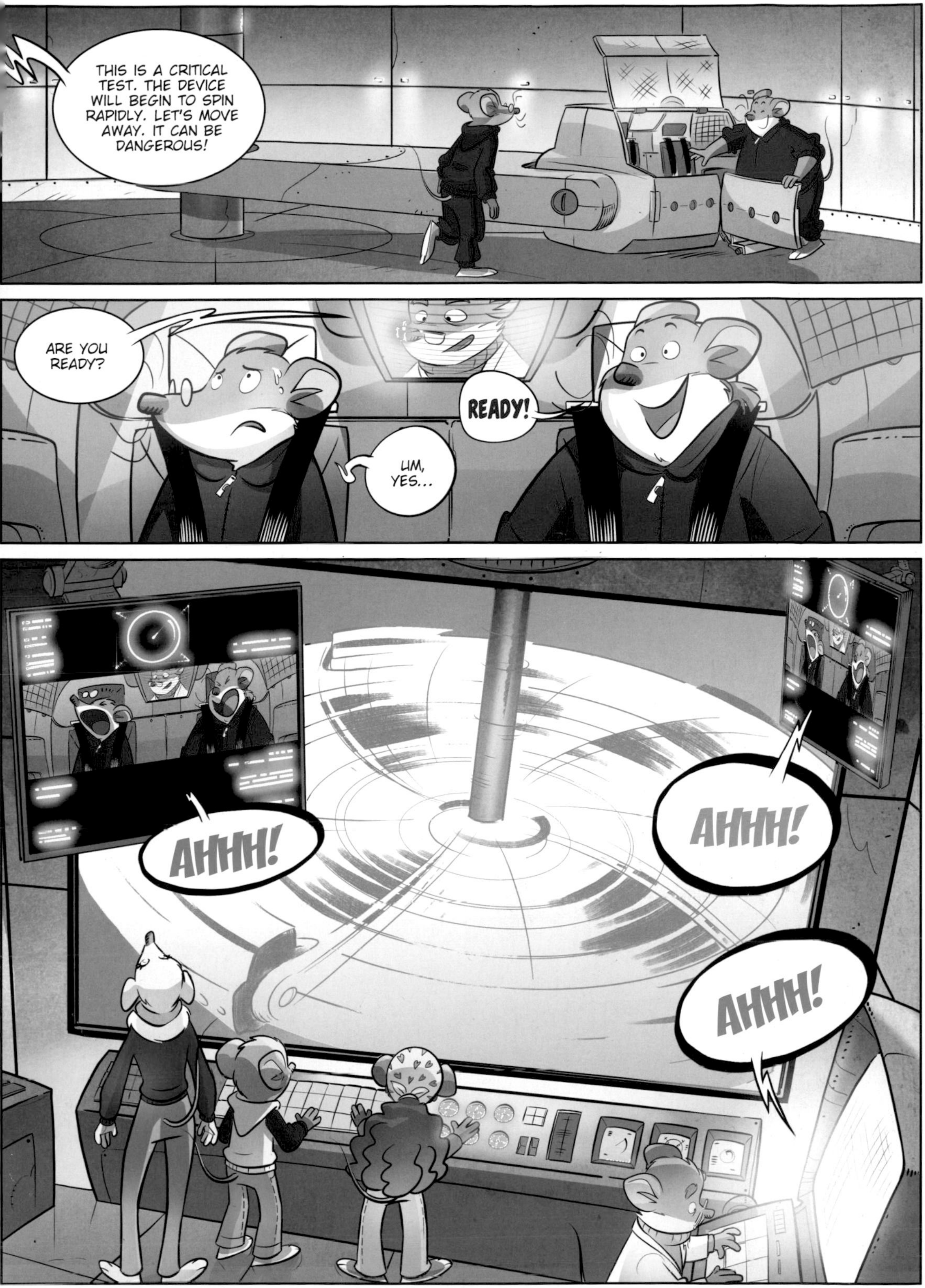
THIS IS A CRITICAL TEST. THE DEVICE WILL BEGIN TO SPIN RAPIDLY. LET'S MOVE AWAY. IT CAN BE DANGEROUS!
ARE YOU READY?
UM, YES...
READY!
AHHH!
AHHH!
AHHH!

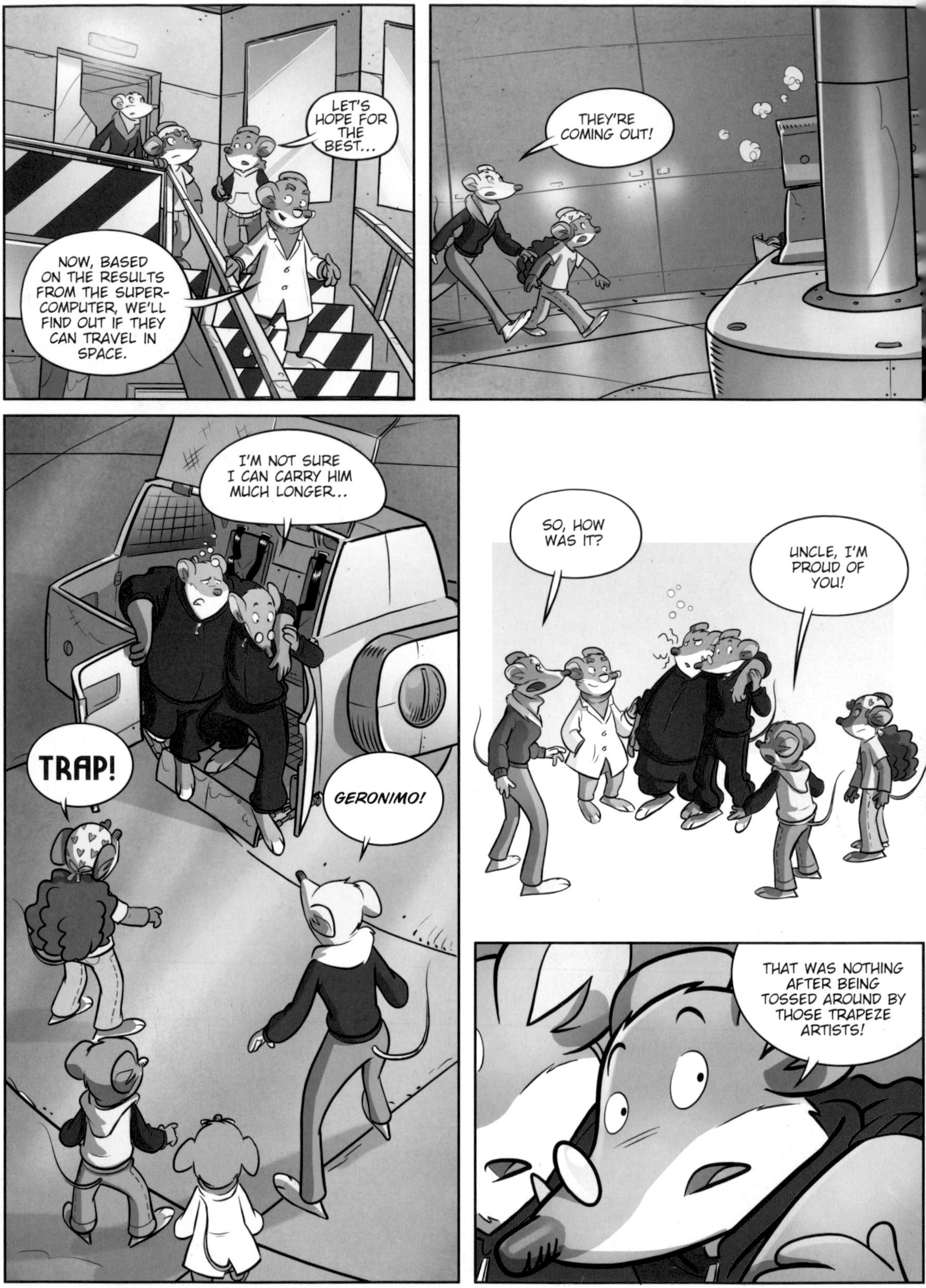
LET'S HOPE FOR THE BEST...
NOW, BASED ON THE RESULTS FROM THE SUPER-COMPUTER, WE'LL FIND OUT IF THEY CAN TRAVEL IN SPACE.
THEY'RE COMING OUT!
I'M NOT SURE I CAN CARRY HIM MUCH LONGER...
TRAP!
GERONIMO!
SO, HOW WAS IT?
UNCLE, I'M PROUD OF YOU!
THAT WAS NOTHING AFTER BEING TOSSED AROUND BY THOSE TRAPEZE ARTISTS!

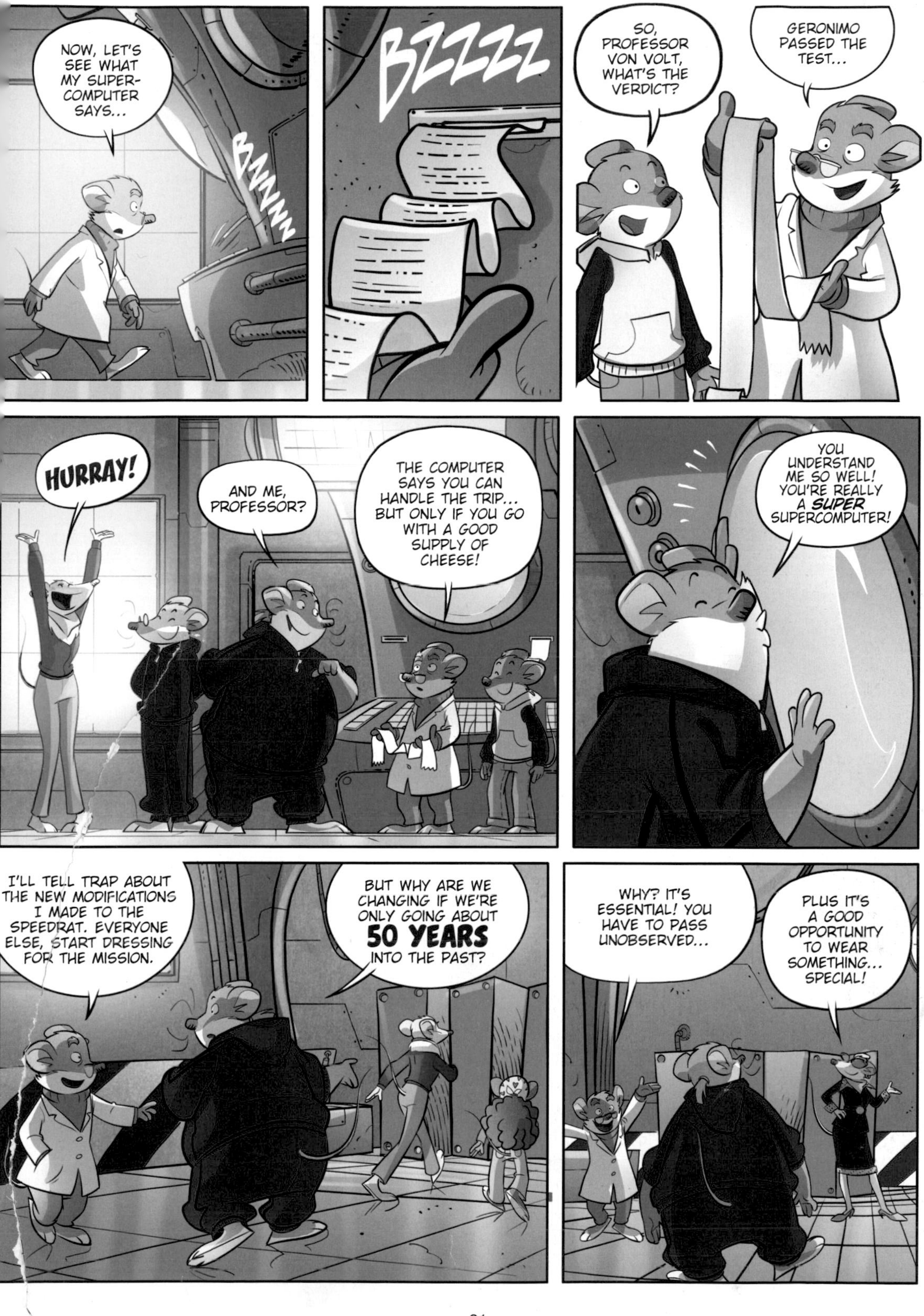
NOW, LET'S SEE WHAT MY SUPER-COMPUTER SAYS...
BZZZZ
BZZZZZ
SO, PROFESSOR VON VOLT, WHAT'S THE VERDICT?
GERONIMO PASSED THE TEST...
HURRAY!
AND ME, PROFESSOR?
THE COMPUTER SAYS YOU CAN HANDLE THE TRIP... BUT ONLY IF YOU GO WITH A GOOD SUPPLY OF CHEESE!
YOU UNDERSTAND ME SO WELL! YOU'RE REALLY A SUPER SUPERCOMPUTER!
I'LL TELL TRAP ABOUT THE NEW MODIFICATIONS I MADE TO THE SPEEDRAT. EVERYONE ELSE, START DRESSING FOR THE MISSION.
BUT WHY ARE WE CHANGING IF WE'RE ONLY GOING ABOUT 50 YEARS INTO THE PAST?
WHY? IT'S ESSENTIAL! YOU HAVE TO PASS UNOBSERVED...
PLUS IT'S A GOOD OPPORTUNITY TO WEAR SOMETHING... SPECIAL!

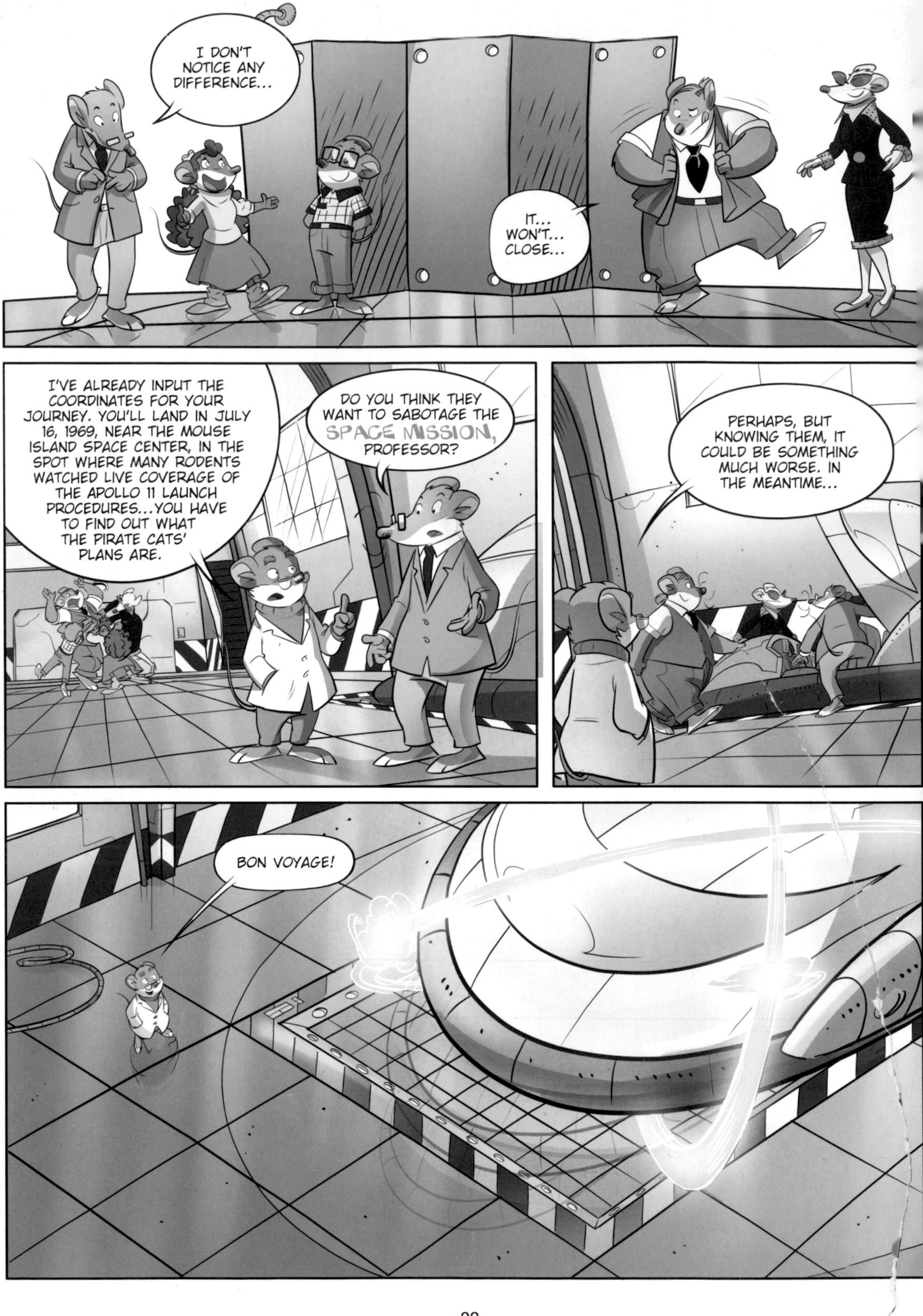
I DON'T NOTICE ANY DIFFERENCE...
IT... WON'T... CLOSE...
I'VE ALREADY INPUT THE COORDINATES FOR YOUR JOURNEY. YOU'LL LAND IN JULY 16, 1969, NEAR THE MOUSE ISLAND SPACE CENTER, IN THE SPOT WHERE MANY RODENTS WATCHED LIVE COVERAGE OF THE APOLLO 11 LAUNCH PROCEDURES...YOU HAVE TO FIND OUT WHAT THE PIRATE CATS' PLANS ARE.
DO YOU THINK THEY WANT TO SABOTAGE THE SPACE MISSION, PROFESSOR?
PERHAPS, BUT KNOWING THEM, IT COULD BE SOMETHING MUCH WORSE. IN THE MEANTIME...
BON VOYAGE!

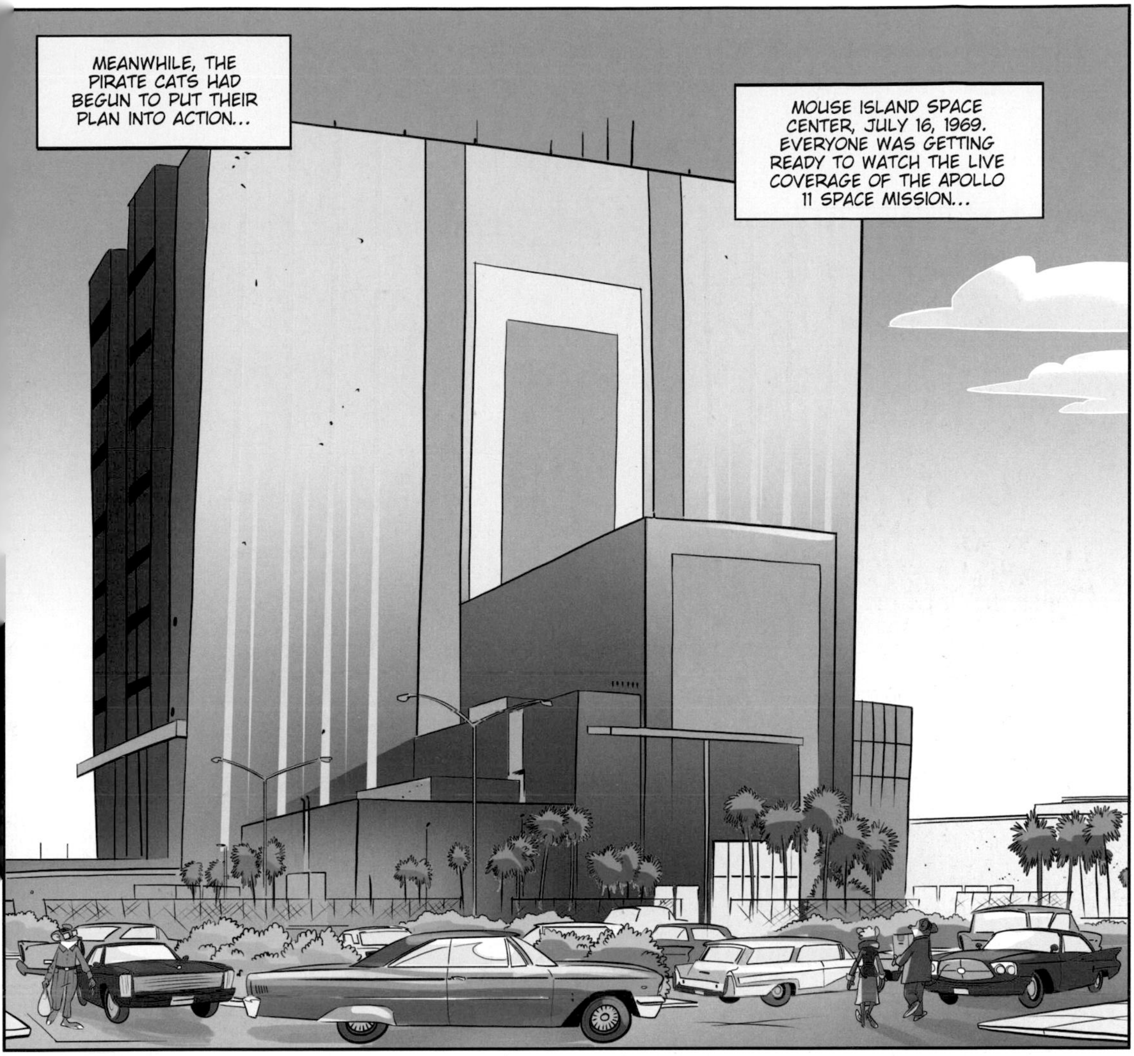
MEANWHILE, THE PIRATE CATS HAD BEGUN TO PUT THEIR PLAN INTO ACTION...
MOUSE ISLAND SPACE CENTER, JULY 16, 1969. EVERYONE WAS GETTING READY TO WATCH THE LIVE COVERAGE OF THE APOLLO 11 SPACE MISSION...

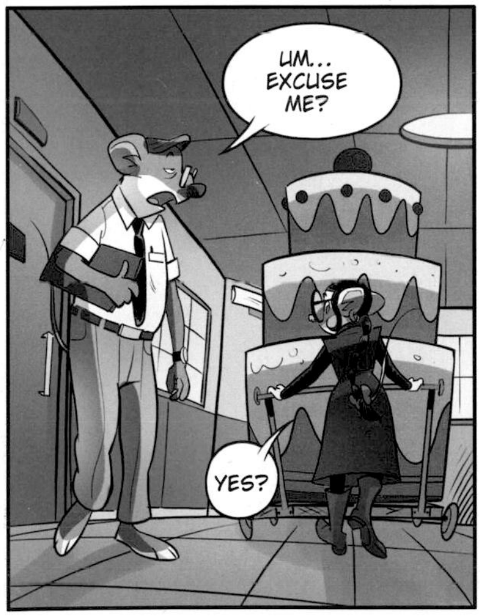
UM... EXCUSE ME?
YES?

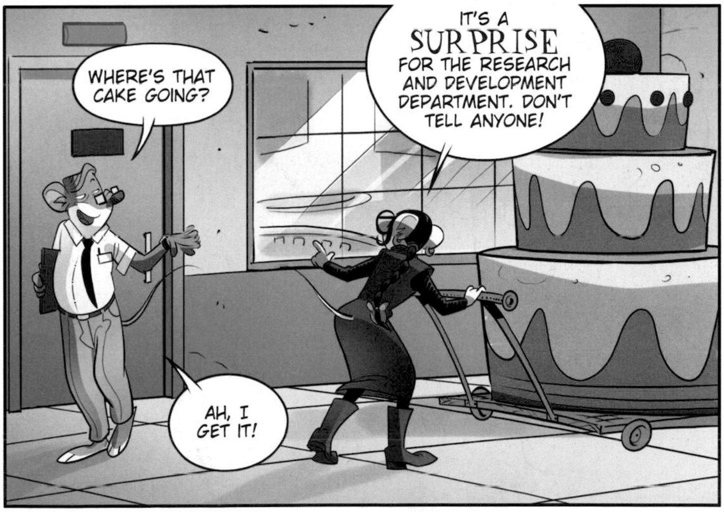
WHERE'S THAT CAKE GOING?
IT'S A SURPRISE FOR THE RESEARCH AND DEVELOPMENT DEPARTMENT. DON'T TELL ANYONE!
AH, I GET IT!

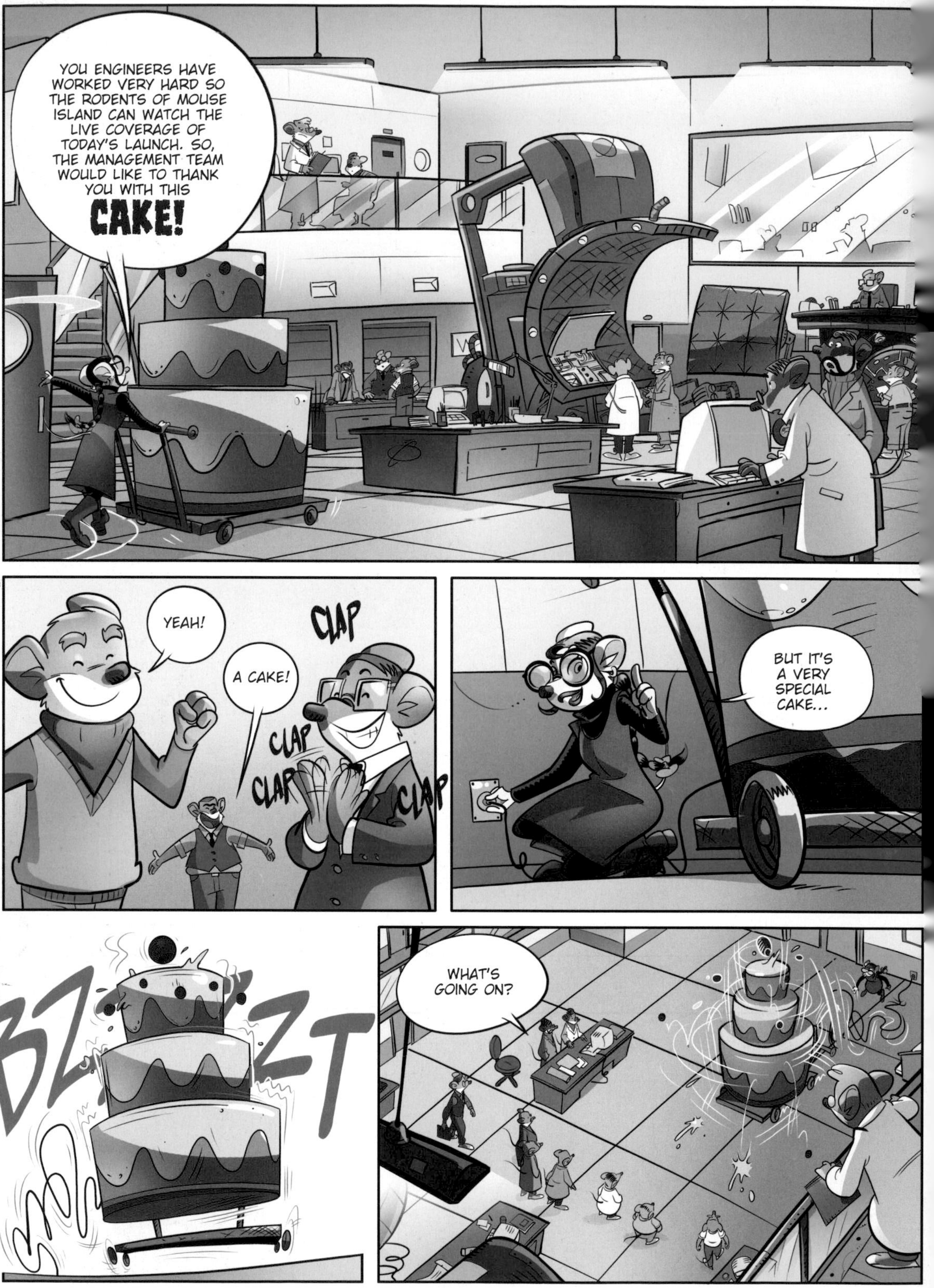
YOU ENGINEERS HAVE WORKED VERY HARD SO THE RODENTS OF MOUSE ISLAND CAN WATCH THE LIVE COVERAGE OF TODAY'S LAUNCH. SO, THE MANAGEMENT TEAM WOULD LIKE TO THANK YOU WITH THIS CAKE!
YEAH!
CLAP
A CAKE!
CLAP
CLAP
CLAP
BUT IT'S A VERY SPECIAL CAKE...
BZZZZT
WHAT'S GOING ON?

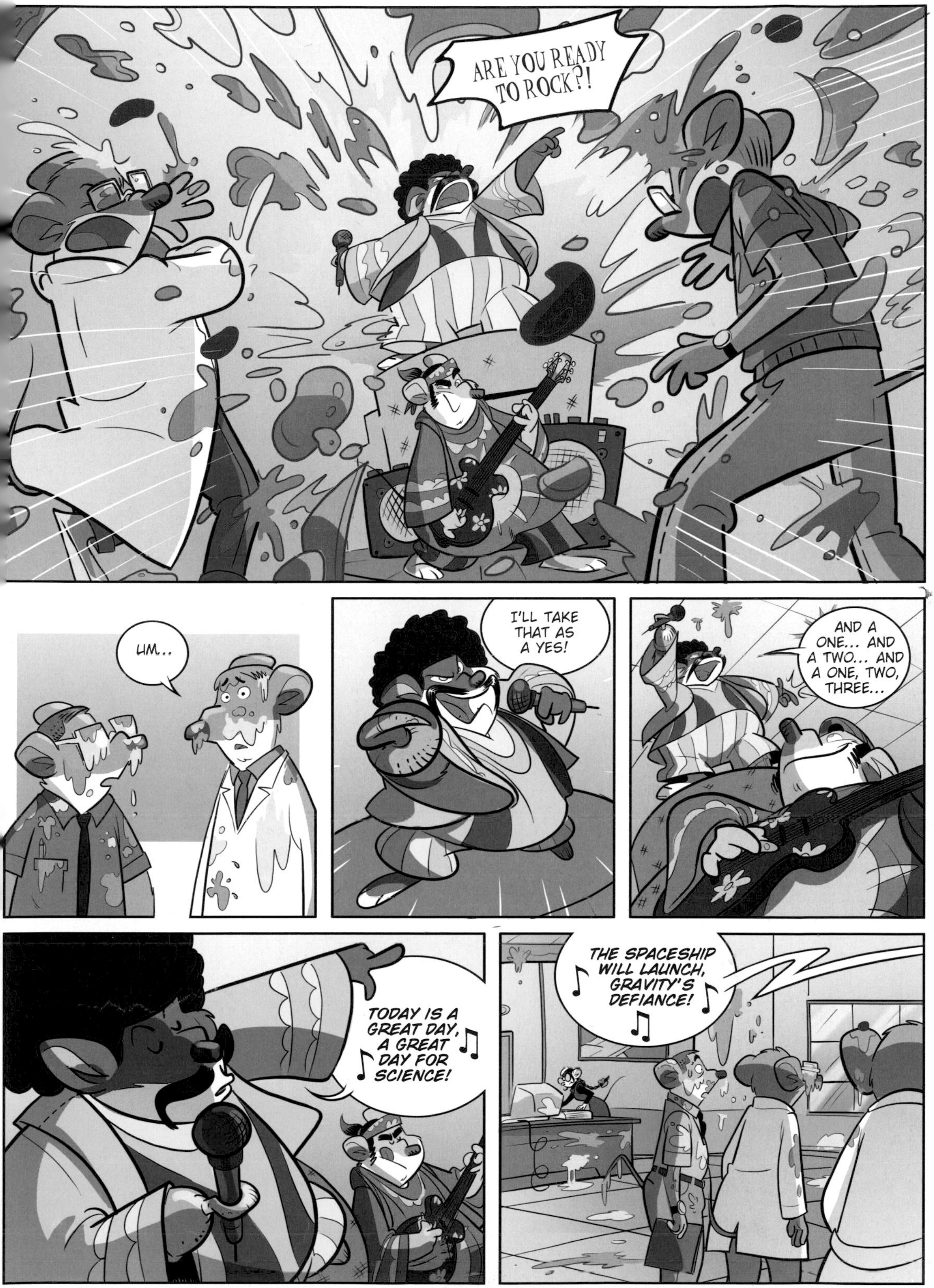
ARE YOU READY TO ROCK?!
UM...
I'LL TAKE THAT AS A YES!
AND A ONE... AND A TWO... AND A ONE, TWO, THREE...
TODAY IS A GREAT DAY, A GREAT DAY FOR SCIENCE!
THE SPACESHIP WILL LAUNCH, GRAVITY'S DEFIANCE!

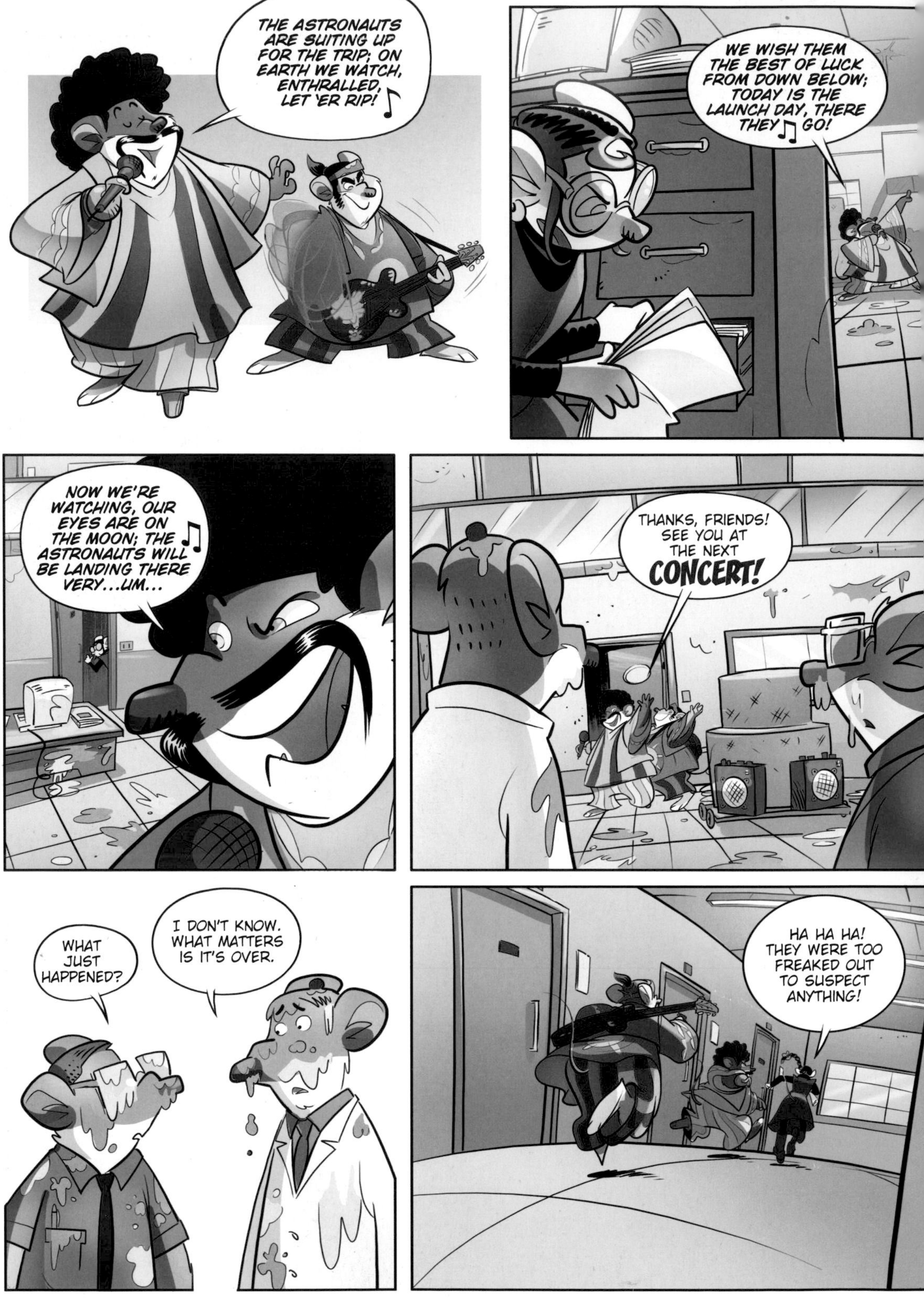
THE ASTRONAUTS ARE SUITING UP FOR THE TRIP; ON EARTH WE WATCH, ENTHRALLED, LET 'ER RIP!
WE WISH THEM THE BEST OF LUCK FROM DOWN BELOW; TODAY IS THE LAUNCH DAY, THERE THEY GO!
NOW WE'RE WATCHING, OUR EYES ARE ON THE MOON; THE ASTRONAUTS WILL BE LANDING THERE VERY...UM...
THANKS, FRIENDS! SEE YOU AT THE NEXT CONCERT!
WHAT JUST HAPPENED?
I DON'T KNOW. WHAT MATTERS IS IT'S OVER.
HA HA HA! THEY WERE TOO FREAKED OUT TO SUSPECT ANYTHING!

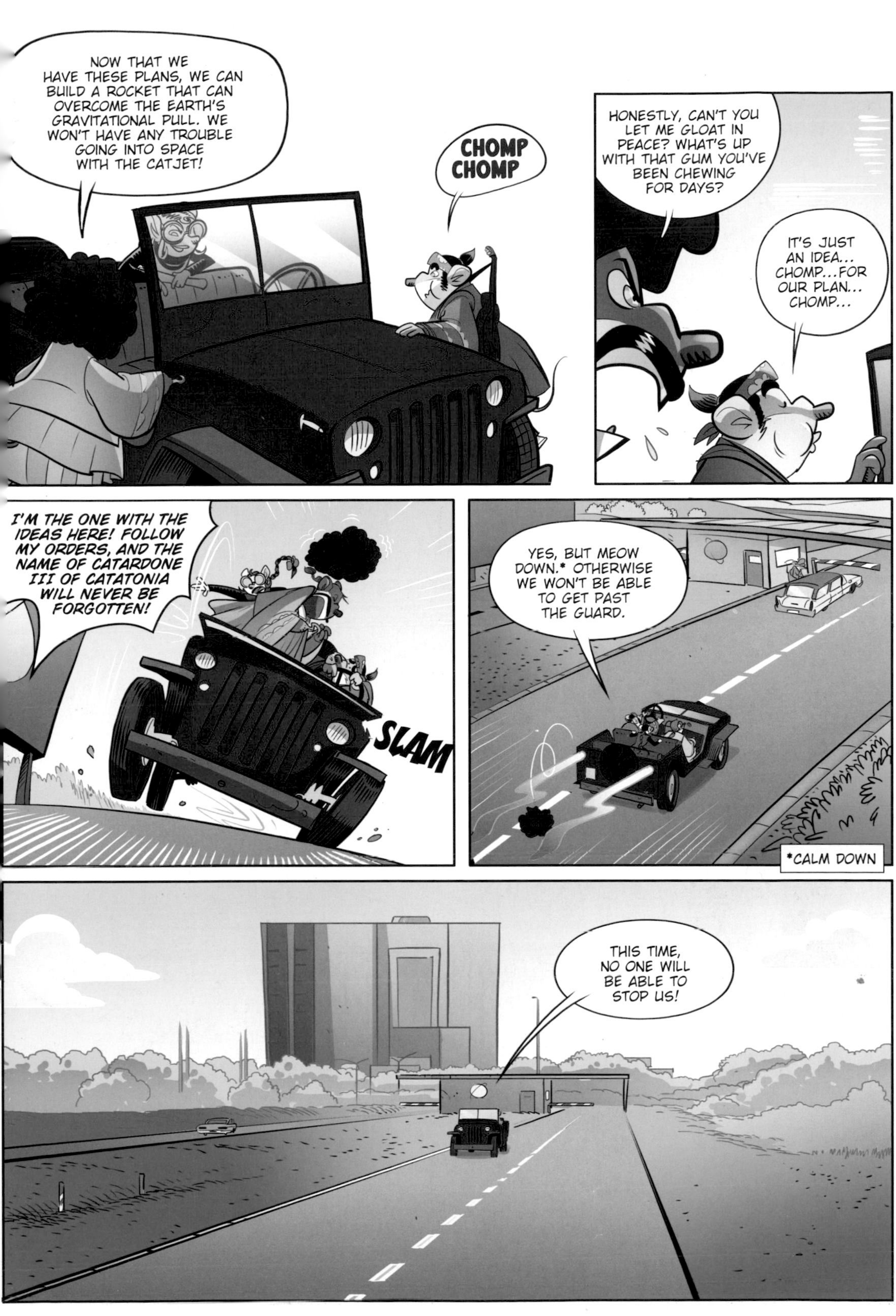
NOW THAT WE HAVE THESE PLANS, WE CAN BUILD A ROCKET THAT CAN OVERCOME THE EARTH'S GRAVITATIONAL PULL. WE WON'T HAVE ANY TROUBLE GOING INTO SPACE WITH THE CATJET!
CHOMP CHOMP
HONESTLY, CAN'T YOU LET ME GLOAT IN PEACE? WHAT'S UP WITH THAT GUM YOU'VE BEEN CHEWING FOR DAYS?
IT'S JUST AN IDEA... CHOMP...FOR OUR PLAN... CHOMP...
I'M THE ONE WITH THE IDEAS HERE! FOLLOW MY ORDERS, AND THE NAME OF CATARDONE III OF CATATONIA WILL NEVER BE FORGOTTEN!
SLAM
YES, BUT MEOW DOWN.* OTHERWISE WE WON'T BE ABLE TO GET PAST THE GUARD.
*CALM DOWN
THIS TIME, NO ONE WILL BE ABLE TO STOP US!

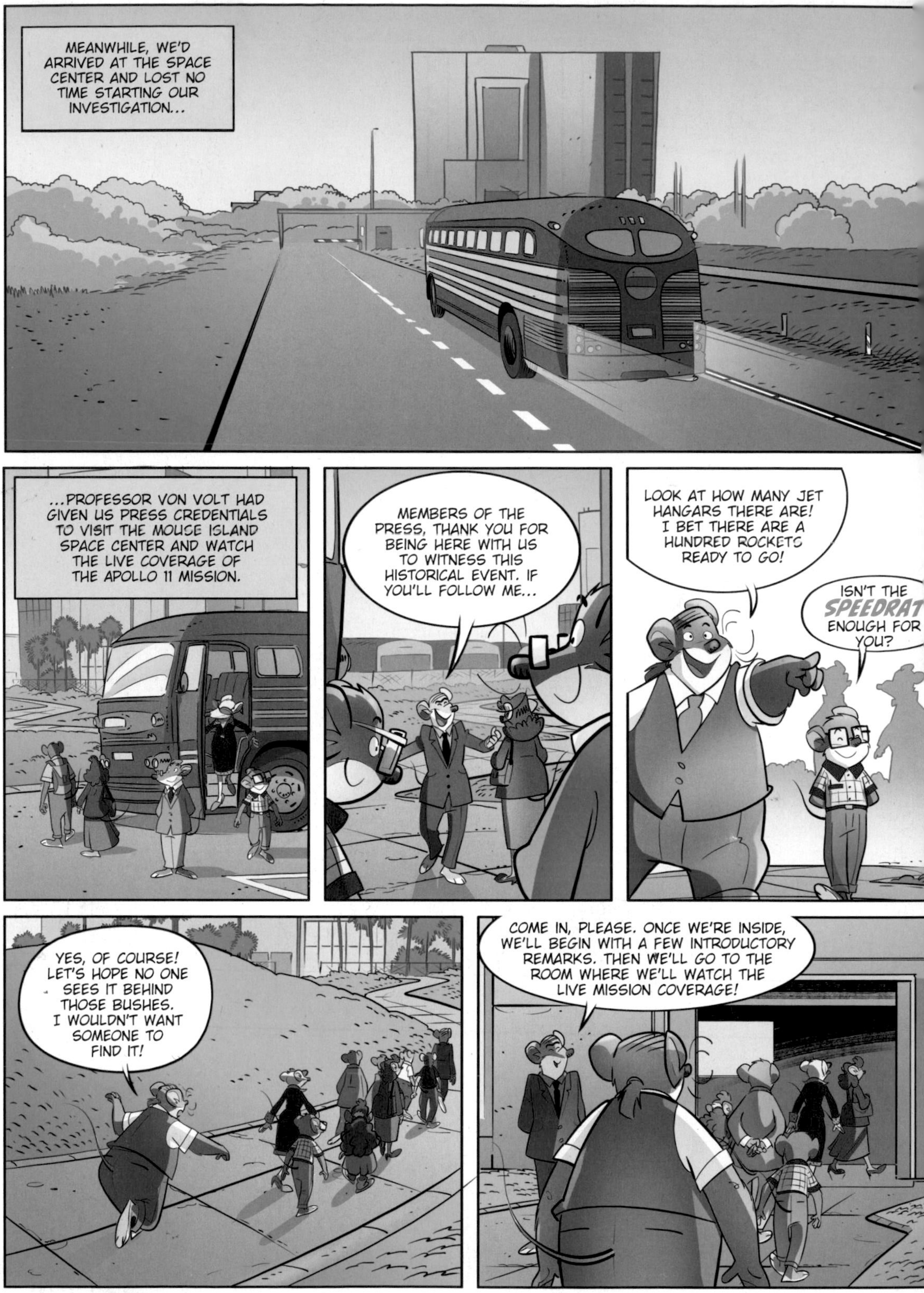

MEANWHILE, WE'D ARRIVED AT THE SPACE CENTER AND LOST NO TIME STARTING OUR INVESTIGATION...
...PROFESSOR VON VOLT HAD GIVEN US PRESS CREDENTIALS TO VISIT THE MOUSE ISLAND SPACE CENTER AND WATCH THE LIVE COVERAGE OF THE APOLLO 11 MISSION.
MEMBERS OF THE PRESS, THANK YOU FOR BEING HERE WITH US TO WITNESS THIS HISTORICAL EVENT. IF YOU'LL FOLLOW ME...
LOOK AT HOW MANY JET HANGARS THERE ARE! I BET THERE ARE A HUNDRED ROCKETS READY TO GO!
ISN'T THE SPEEDRAT ENOUGH FOR YOU?
YES, OF COURSE! LET'S HOPE NO ONE SEES IT BEHIND THOSE BUSHES. I WOULDN'T WANT SOMEONE TO FIND IT!
COME IN, PLEASE. ONCE WE'RE INSIDE, WE'LL BEGIN WITH A FEW INTRODUCTORY REMARKS. THEN WE'LL GO TO THE ROOM WHERE WE'LL WATCH THE LIVE MISSION COVERAGE!

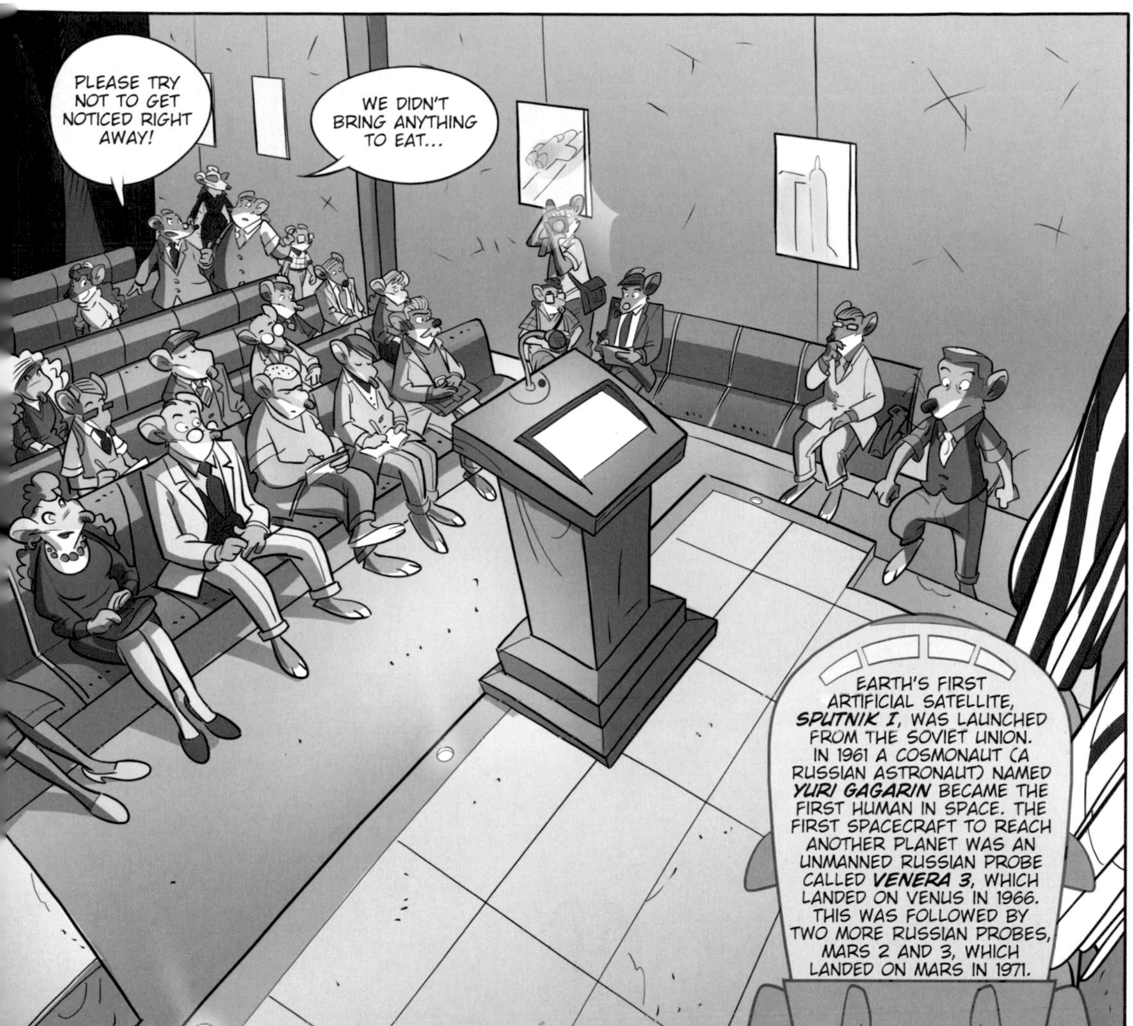
PLEASE TRY NOT TO GET NOTICED RIGHT AWAY!
WE DIDN'T BRING ANYTHING TO EAT...
EARTH'S FIRST ARTIFICIAL SATELLITE, SPUTNIK I, WAS LAUNCHED FROM THE SOVIET UNION. IN 1961 A COSMONAUT (A RUSSIAN ASTRONAUT) NAMED YURI GAGARIN BECAME THE FIRST HUMAN IN SPACE. THE FIRST SPACECRAFT TO REACH ANOTHER PLANET WAS AN UNMANNED RUSSIAN PROBE CALLED VENERA 3, WHICH LANDED ON VENUS IN 1966. THIS WAS FOLLOWED BY TWO MORE RUSSIAN PROBES, MARS 2 AND 3, WHICH LANDED ON MARS IN 1971.

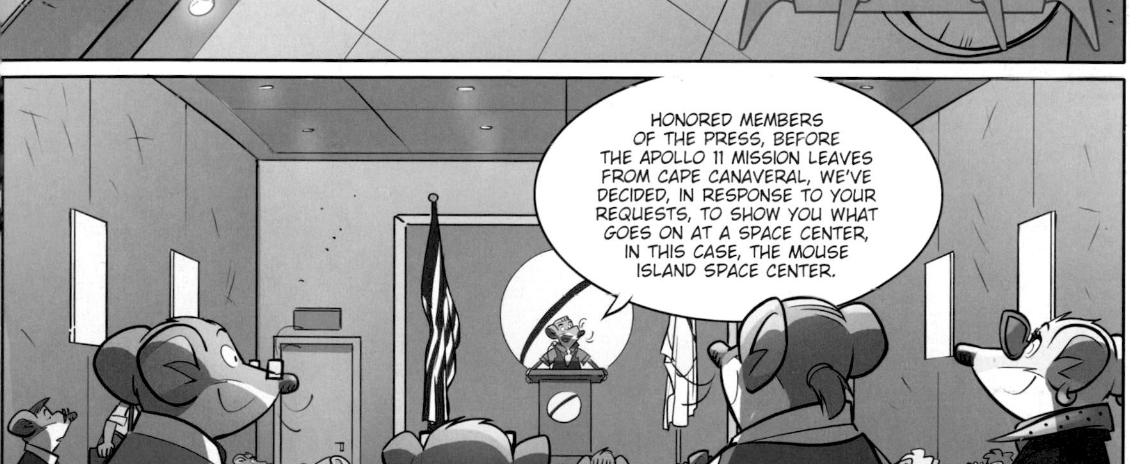
HONORED MEMBERS OF THE PRESS, BEFORE THE APOLLO 11 MISSION LEAVES FROM CAPE CANAVERAL, WE'VE DECIDED, IN RESPONSE TO YOUR REQUESTS, TO SHOW YOU WHAT GOES ON AT A SPACE CENTER, IN THIS CASE, THE MOUSE ISLAND SPACE CENTER.

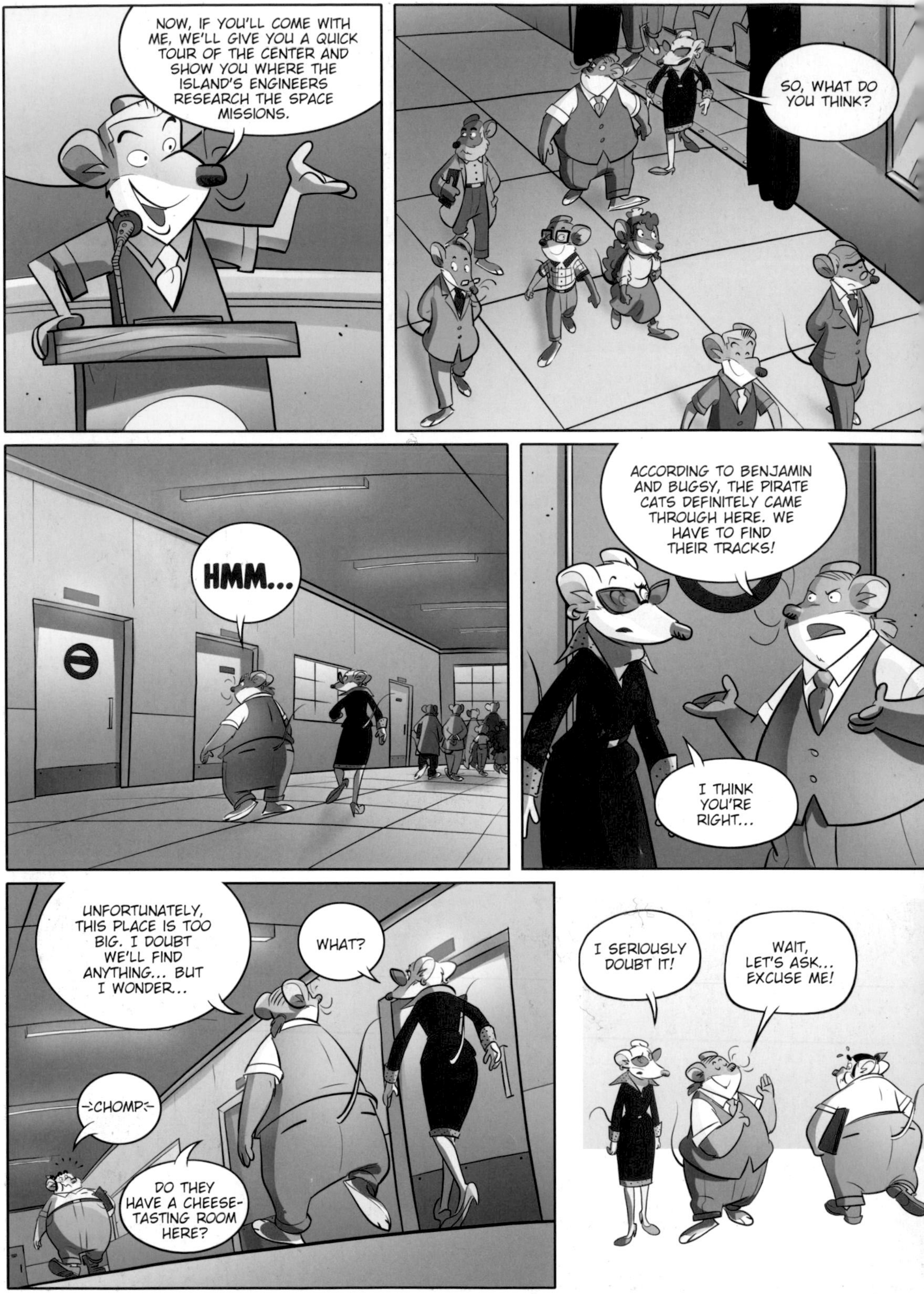
NOW, IF YOU'LL COME WITH ME, WE'LL GIVE YOU A QUICK TOUR OF THE CENTER AND SHOW YOU WHERE THE ISLAND'S ENGINEERS RESEARCH THE SPACE MISSIONS.
SO, WHAT DO YOU THINK?
HMM...
ACCORDING TO BENJAMIN AND BUGSY, THE PIRATE CATS DEFINITELY CAME THROUGH HERE. WE HAVE TO FIND THEIR TRACKS!
I THINK YOU'RE RIGHT...
UNFORTUNATELY, THIS PLACE IS TOO BIG. I DOUBT WE'LL FIND ANYTHING... BUT I WONDER...
WHAT?
CHOMP
DO THEY HAVE A CHEESE-TASTING ROOM HERE?
I SERIOUSLY DOUBT IT!
WAIT, LET'S ASK... EXCUSE ME!

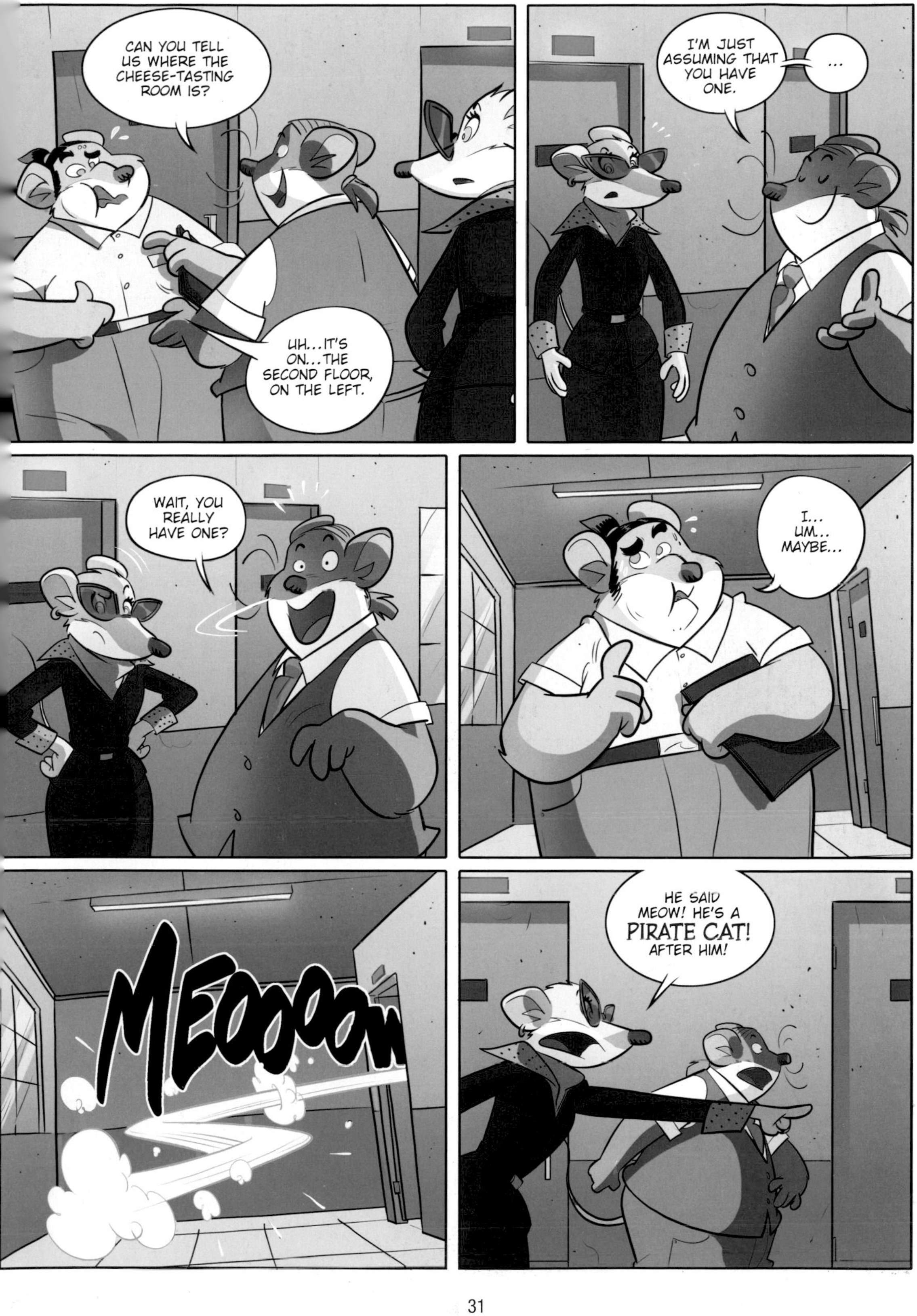
CAN YOU TELL US WHERE THE CHEESE-TASTING ROOM IS?
UH...IT'S ON...THE SECOND FLOOR, ON THE LEFT.
I'M JUST ASSUMING THAT YOU HAVE ONE.
...
WAIT, YOU REALLY HAVE ONE?
I... UM... MAYBE...
MEOOOOW
HE SAID MEOW! HE'S A PIRATE CAT! AFTER HIM!

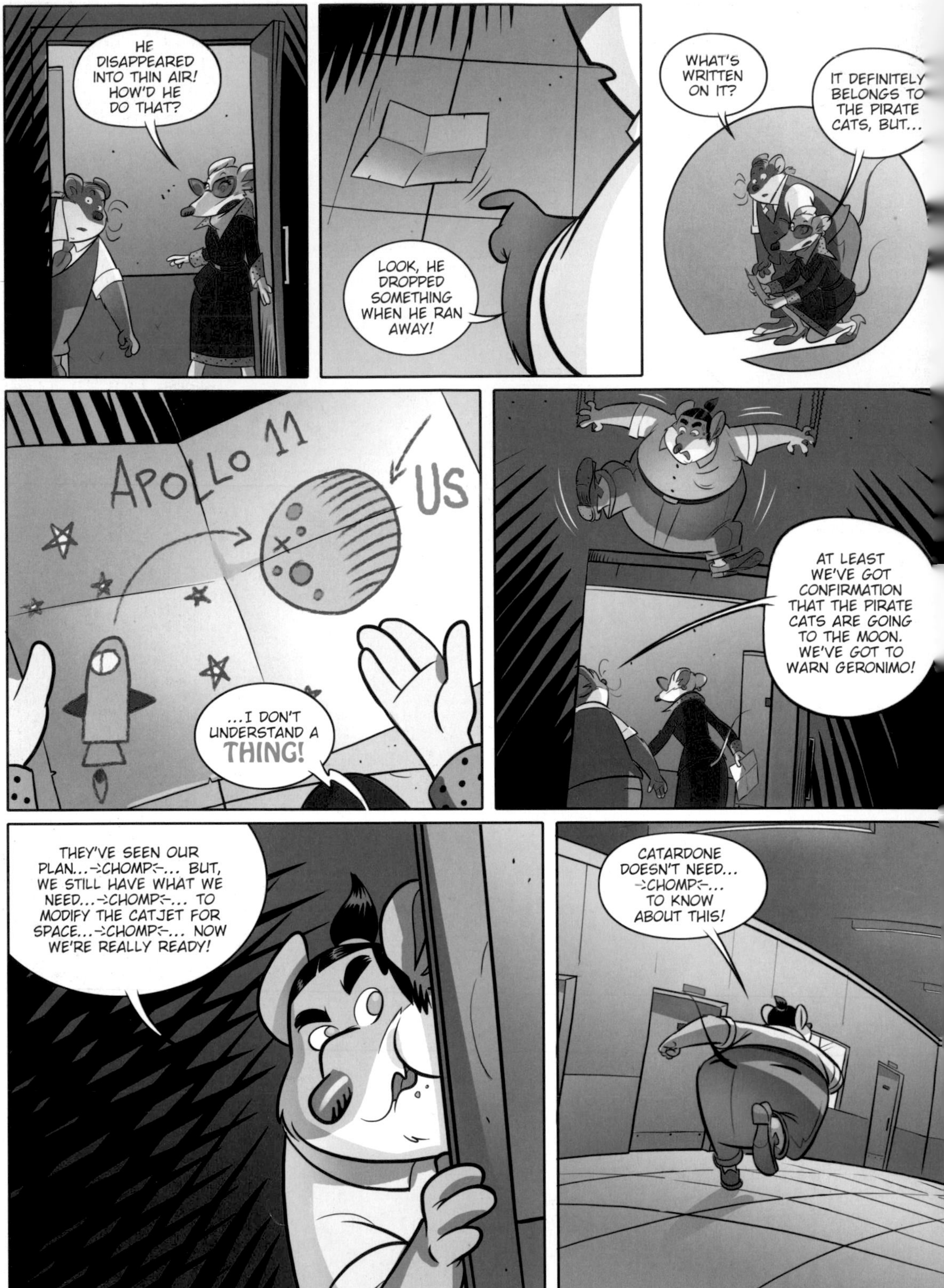
HE DISAPPEARED INTO THIN AIR! HOW'D HE DO THAT?
LOOK, HE DROPPED SOMETHING WHEN HE RAN AWAY!
WHAT'S WRITTEN ON IT?
IT DEFINITELY BELONGS TO THE PIRATE CATS, BUT...
APOLLO 11
US
...I DON'T UNDERSTAND A THING!
AT LEAST WE'VE GOT CONFIRMATION THAT THE PIRATE CATS ARE GOING TO THE MOON. WE'VE GOT TO WARN GERONIMO!
THEY'VE SEEN OUR PLAN... ⇢CHOMP⇠... BUT, WE STILL HAVE WHAT WE NEED... ⇢CHOMP⇠... TO MODIFY THE CATJET FOR SPACE... ⇢CHOMP⇠... NOW WE'RE REALLY READY!
CATARDONE DOESN'T NEED... ⇢CHOMP⇠... TO KNOW ABOUT THIS!

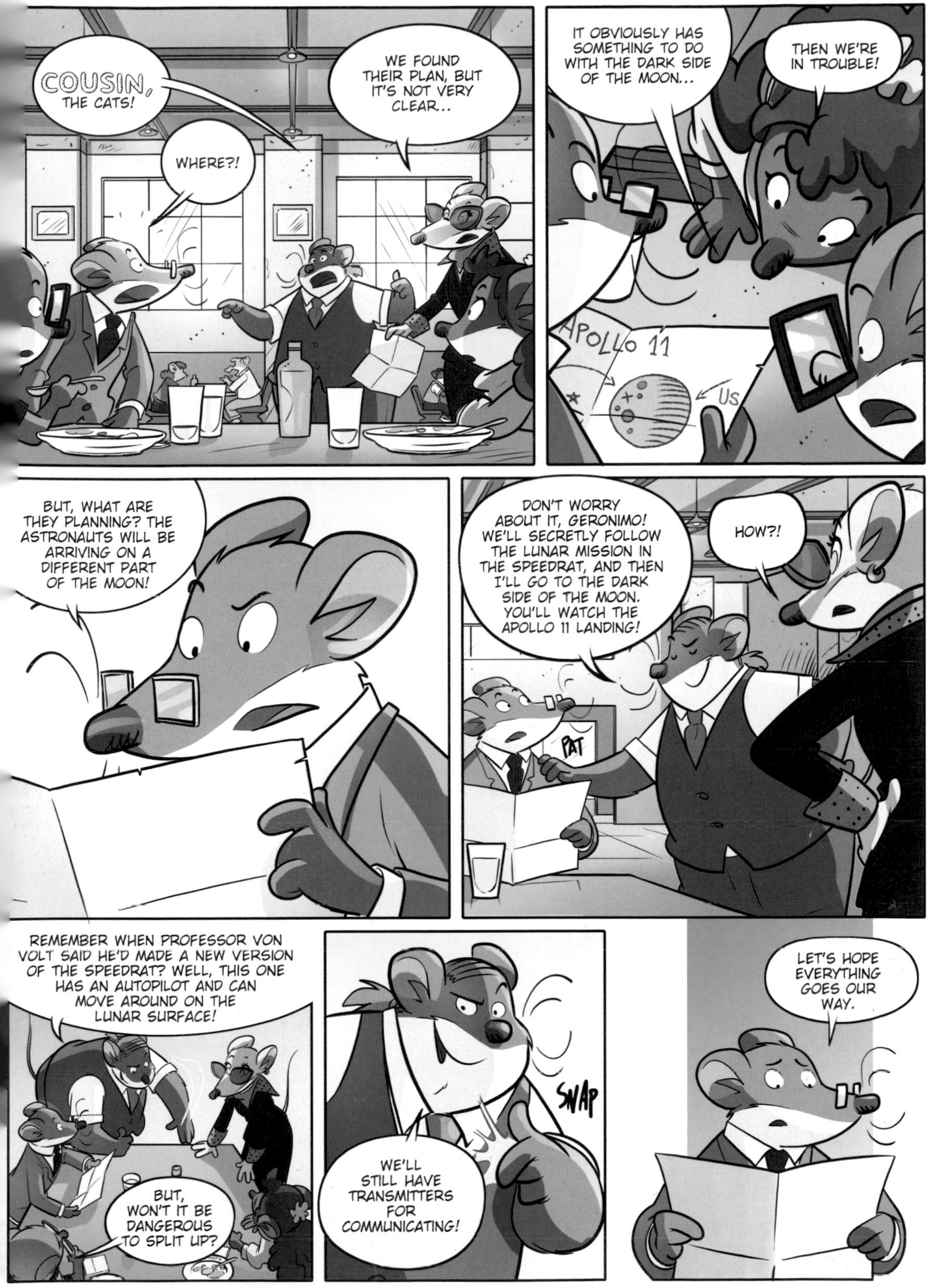

COUSIN, THE CATS!
WHERE?!
WE FOUND THEIR PLAN, BUT IT'S NOT VERY CLEAR...
IT OBVIOUSLY HAS SOMETHING TO DO WITH THE DARK SIDE OF THE MOON...
THEN WE'RE IN TROUBLE!
APOLLO 11
US
BUT, WHAT ARE THEY PLANNING? THE ASTRONAUTS WILL BE ARRIVING ON A DIFFERENT PART OF THE MOON!
DON'T WORRY ABOUT IT, GERONIMO! WE'LL SECRETLY FOLLOW THE LUNAR MISSION IN THE SPEEDRAT, AND THEN I'LL GO TO THE DARK SIDE OF THE MOON. YOU'LL WATCH THE APOLLO 11 LANDING!
HOW?!
PAT
REMEMBER WHEN PROFESSOR VON VOLT SAID HE'D MADE A NEW VERSION OF THE SPEEDRAT? WELL, THIS ONE HAS AN AUTOPILOT AND CAN MOVE AROUND ON THE LUNAR SURFACE!
BUT, WON'T IT BE DANGEROUS TO SPLIT UP?
SNAP
WE'LL STILL HAVE TRANSMITTERS FOR COMMUNICATING!
LET'S HOPE EVERYTHING GOES OUR WAY.

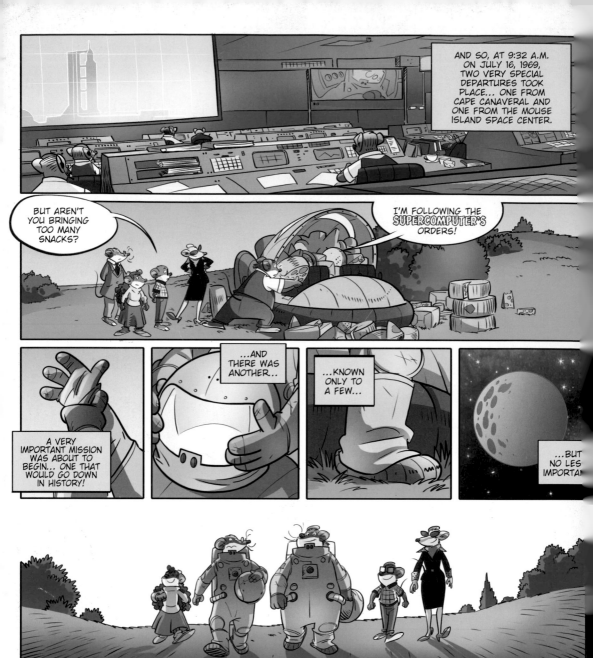

AND SO, AT 9:32 A.M. ON JULY 16, 1969, TWO VERY SPECIAL DEPARTURES TOOK PLACE... ONE FROM CAPE CANAVERAL AND ONE FROM THE MOUSE ISLAND SPACE CENTER.

BUT AREN'T YOU BRINGING TOO MANY SNACKS?

I'M FOLLOWING THE **SUPERCOMPUTER'S** ORDERS!

A VERY IMPORTANT MISSION WAS ABOUT TO BEGIN... ONE THAT WOULD GO DOWN IN HISTORY!

...AND THERE WAS ANOTHER...

...KNOWN ONLY TO A FEW...

...BUT NO LES[S] IMPORTA[NT]

THE OFFICIAL MISSION WAS READY TO LEAVE FROM CAPE CANAVERAL.

AND WE WERE, TOO!

34

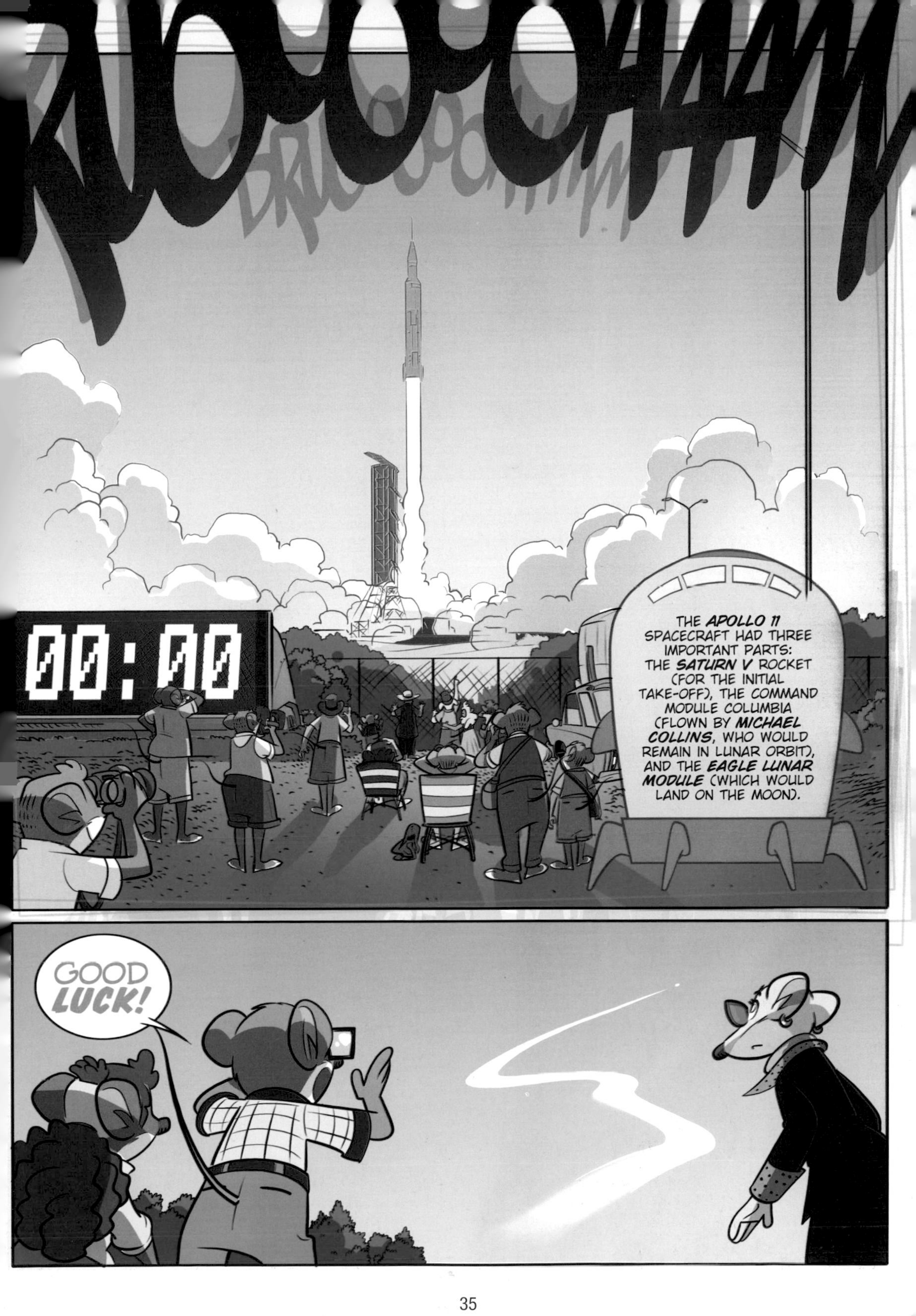
00:00
THE APOLLO 11 SPACECRAFT HAD THREE IMPORTANT PARTS: THE SATURN V ROCKET (FOR THE INITIAL TAKE-OFF), THE COMMAND MODULE COLUMBIA (FLOWN BY MICHAEL COLLINS, WHO WOULD REMAIN IN LUNAR ORBIT), AND THE EAGLE LUNAR MODULE (WHICH WOULD LAND ON THE MOON).
GOOD LUCK!

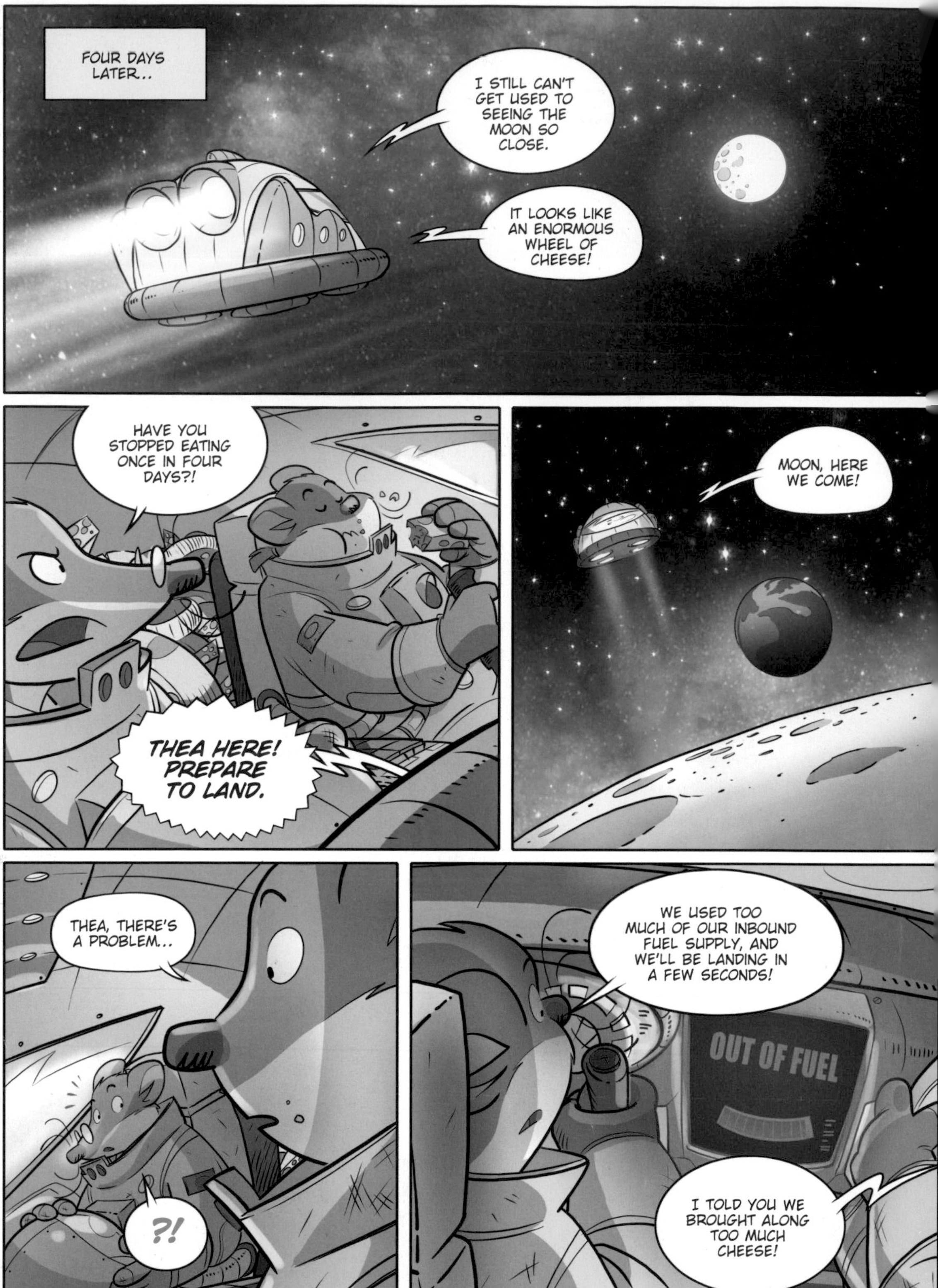
FOUR DAYS LATER...
I STILL CAN'T GET USED TO SEEING THE MOON SO CLOSE.
IT LOOKS LIKE AN ENORMOUS WHEEL OF CHEESE!
HAVE YOU STOPPED EATING ONCE IN FOUR DAYS?!
THEA HERE! PREPARE TO LAND.
MOON, HERE WE COME!
THEA, THERE'S A PROBLEM...
?!
WE USED TOO MUCH OF OUR INBOUND FUEL SUPPLY, AND WE'LL BE LANDING IN A FEW SECONDS!
OUT OF FUEL
I TOLD YOU WE BROUGHT ALONG TOO MUCH CHEESE!

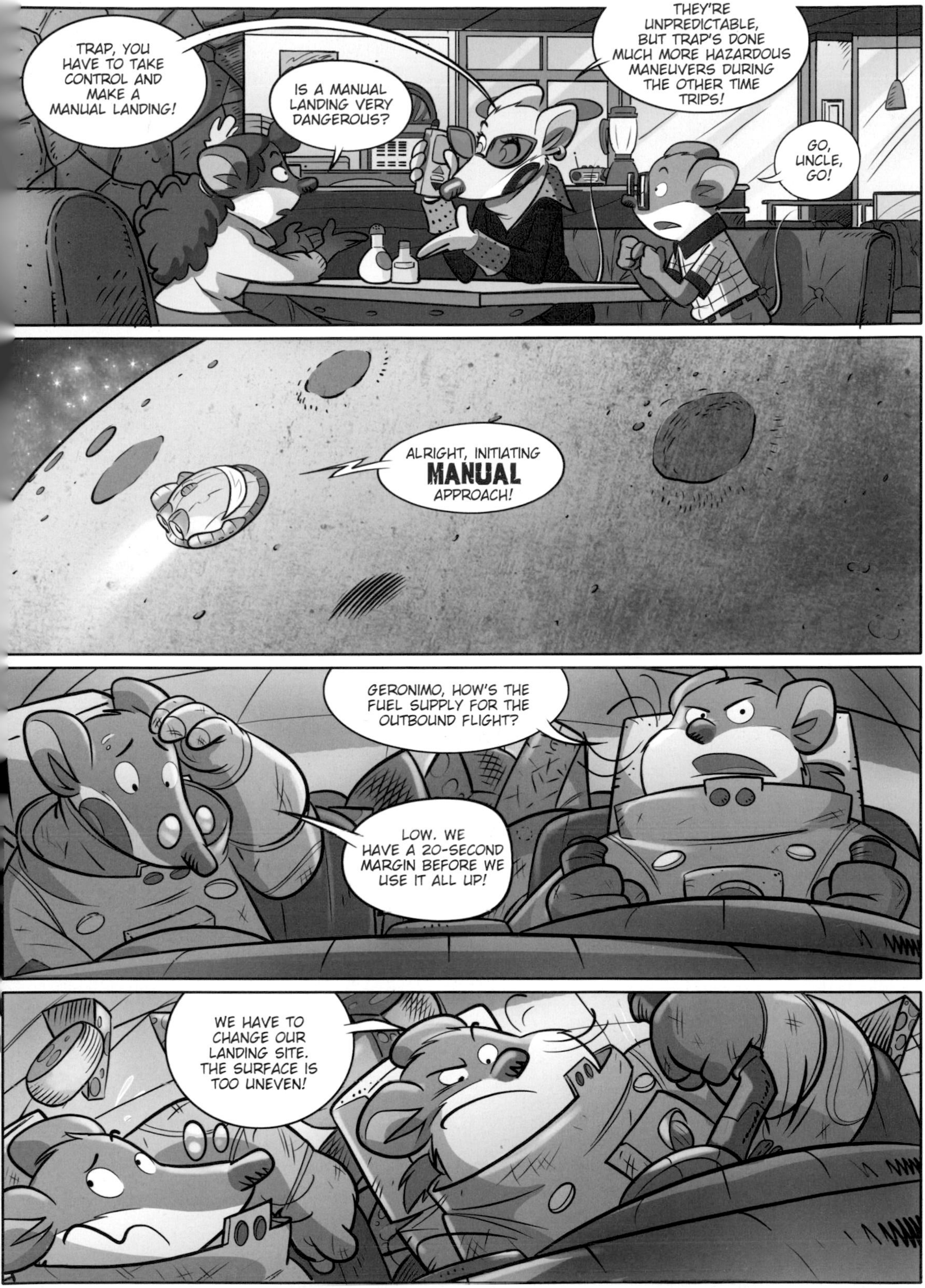
TRAP, YOU HAVE TO TAKE CONTROL AND MAKE A MANUAL LANDING!
IS A MANUAL LANDING VERY DANGEROUS?
THEY'RE UNPREDICTABLE, BUT TRAP'S DONE MUCH MORE HAZARDOUS MANEUVERS DURING THE OTHER TIME TRIPS!
GO, UNCLE, GO!
ALRIGHT, INITIATING MANUAL APPROACH!
GERONIMO, HOW'S THE FUEL SUPPLY FOR THE OUTBOUND FLIGHT?
LOW. WE HAVE A 20-SECOND MARGIN BEFORE WE USE IT ALL UP!
WE HAVE TO CHANGE OUR LANDING SITE. THE SURFACE IS TOO UNEVEN!

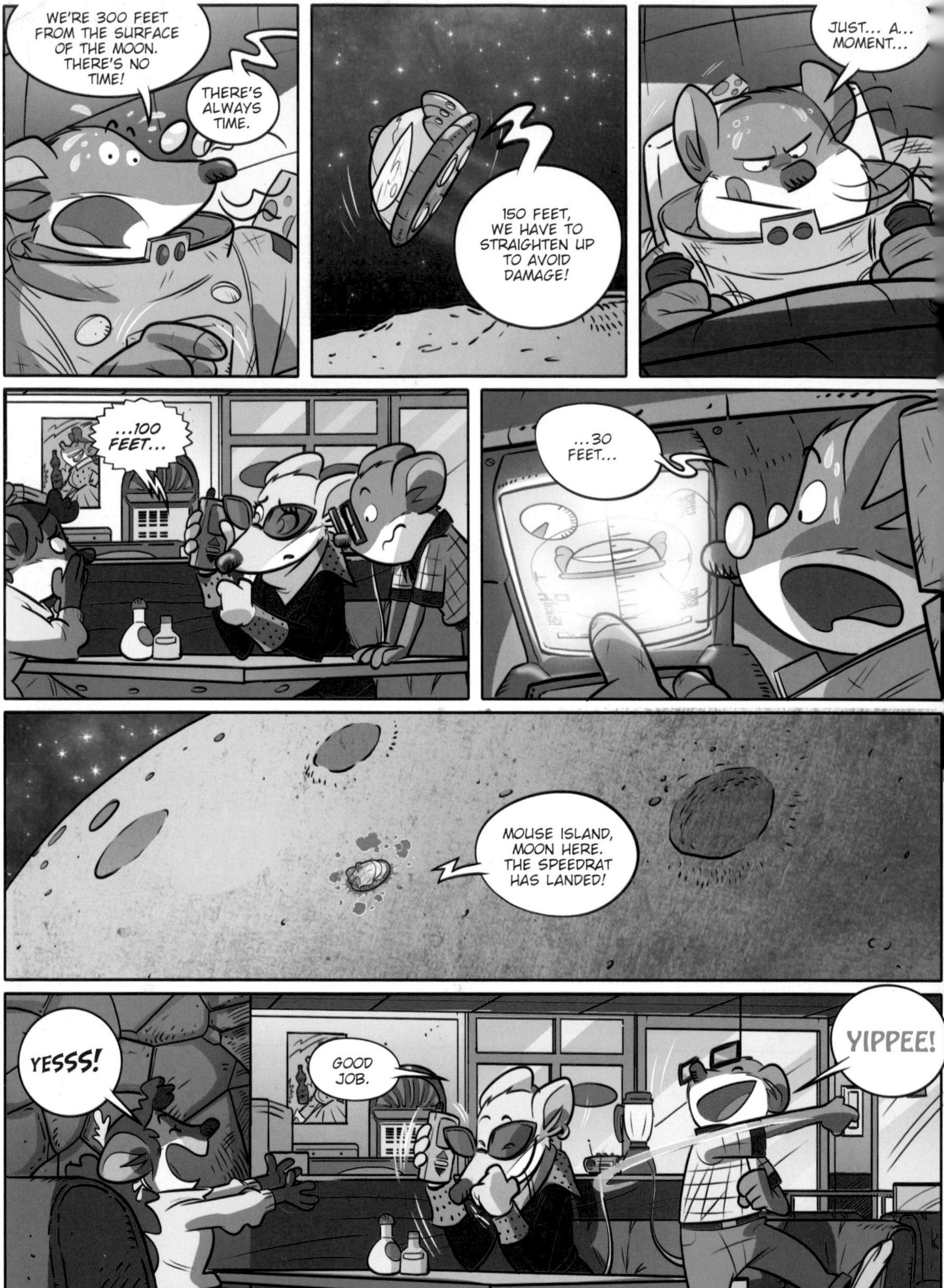
WE'RE 300 FEET FROM THE SURFACE OF THE MOON. THERE'S NO TIME!
THERE'S ALWAYS TIME.
150 FEET, WE HAVE TO STRAIGHTEN UP TO AVOID DAMAGE!
JUST... A... MOMENT...
...100 FEET...
...30 FEET...
MOUSE ISLAND, MOON HERE. THE SPEEDRAT HAS LANDED!
YESSS!
GOOD JOB.
YIPPEE!

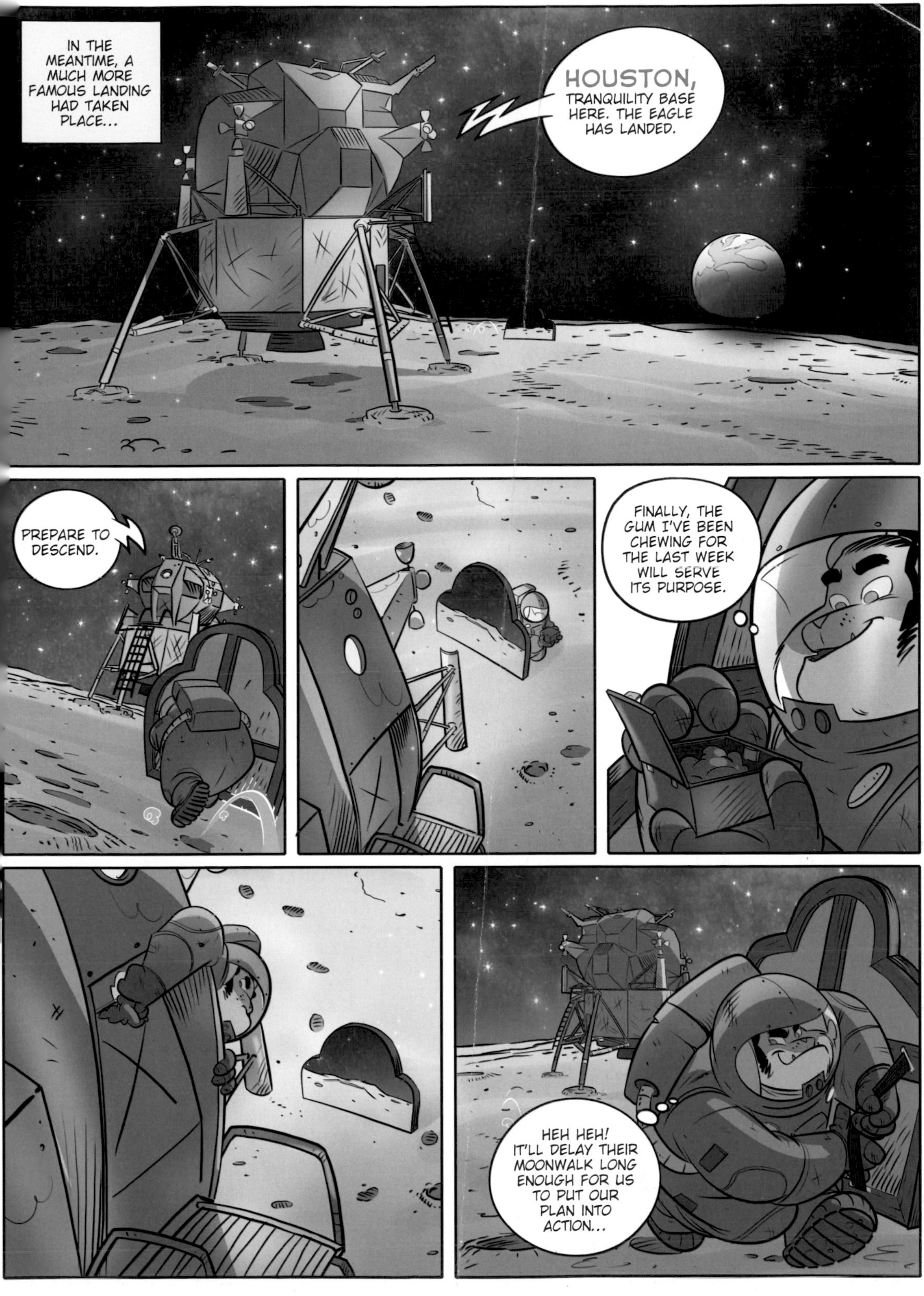
IN THE MEANTIME, A MUCH MORE FAMOUS LANDING HAD TAKEN PLACE...
HOUSTON, TRANQUILITY BASE HERE. THE EAGLE HAS LANDED.
PREPARE TO DESCEND.
FINALLY, THE GUM I'VE BEEN CHEWING FOR THE LAST WEEK WILL SERVE ITS PURPOSE.
HEH HEH! IT'LL DELAY THEIR MOONWALK LONG ENOUGH FOR US TO PUT OUR PLAN INTO ACTION...

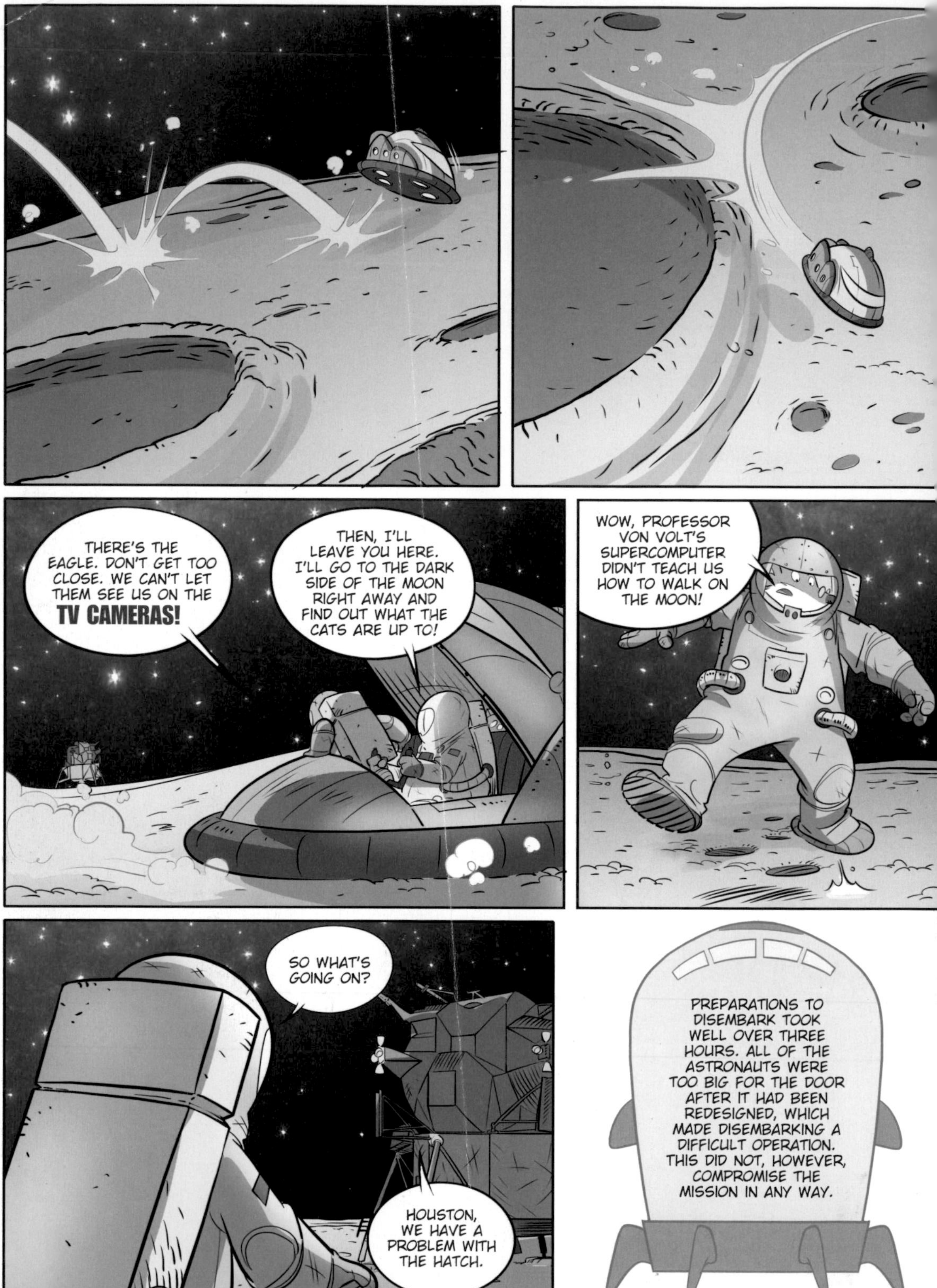

THERE'S THE EAGLE. DON'T GET TOO CLOSE. WE CAN'T LET THEM SEE US ON THE TV CAMERAS!
THEN, I'LL LEAVE YOU HERE. I'LL GO TO THE DARK SIDE OF THE MOON RIGHT AWAY AND FIND OUT WHAT THE CATS ARE UP TO!
WOW, PROFESSOR VON VOLT'S SUPERCOMPUTER DIDN'T TEACH US HOW TO WALK ON THE MOON!
SO WHAT'S GOING ON?
HOUSTON, WE HAVE A PROBLEM WITH THE HATCH.
PREPARATIONS TO DISEMBARK TOOK WELL OVER THREE HOURS. ALL OF THE ASTRONAUTS WERE TOO BIG FOR THE DOOR AFTER IT HAD BEEN REDESIGNED, WHICH MADE DISEMBARKING A DIFFICULT OPERATION. THIS DID NOT, HOWEVER, COMPROMISE THE MISSION IN ANY WAY.

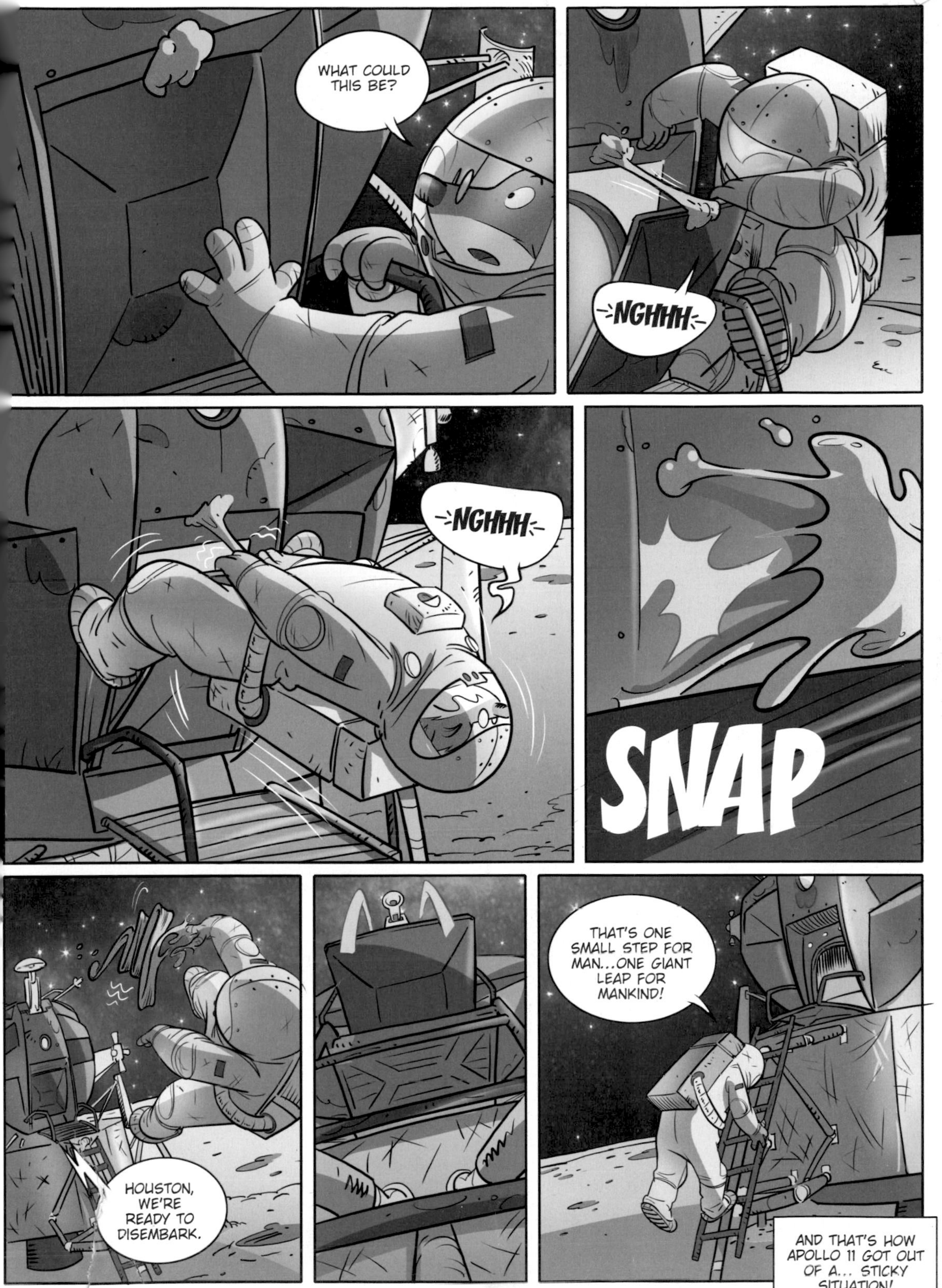
WHAT COULD THIS BE?
NGHHH
NGHHH
SNAP
HOUSTON, WE'RE READY TO DISEMBARK.
THAT'S ONE SMALL STEP FOR MAN...ONE GIANT LEAP FOR MANKIND!
AND THAT'S HOW APOLLO 11 GOT OUT OF A... STICKY SITUATION!

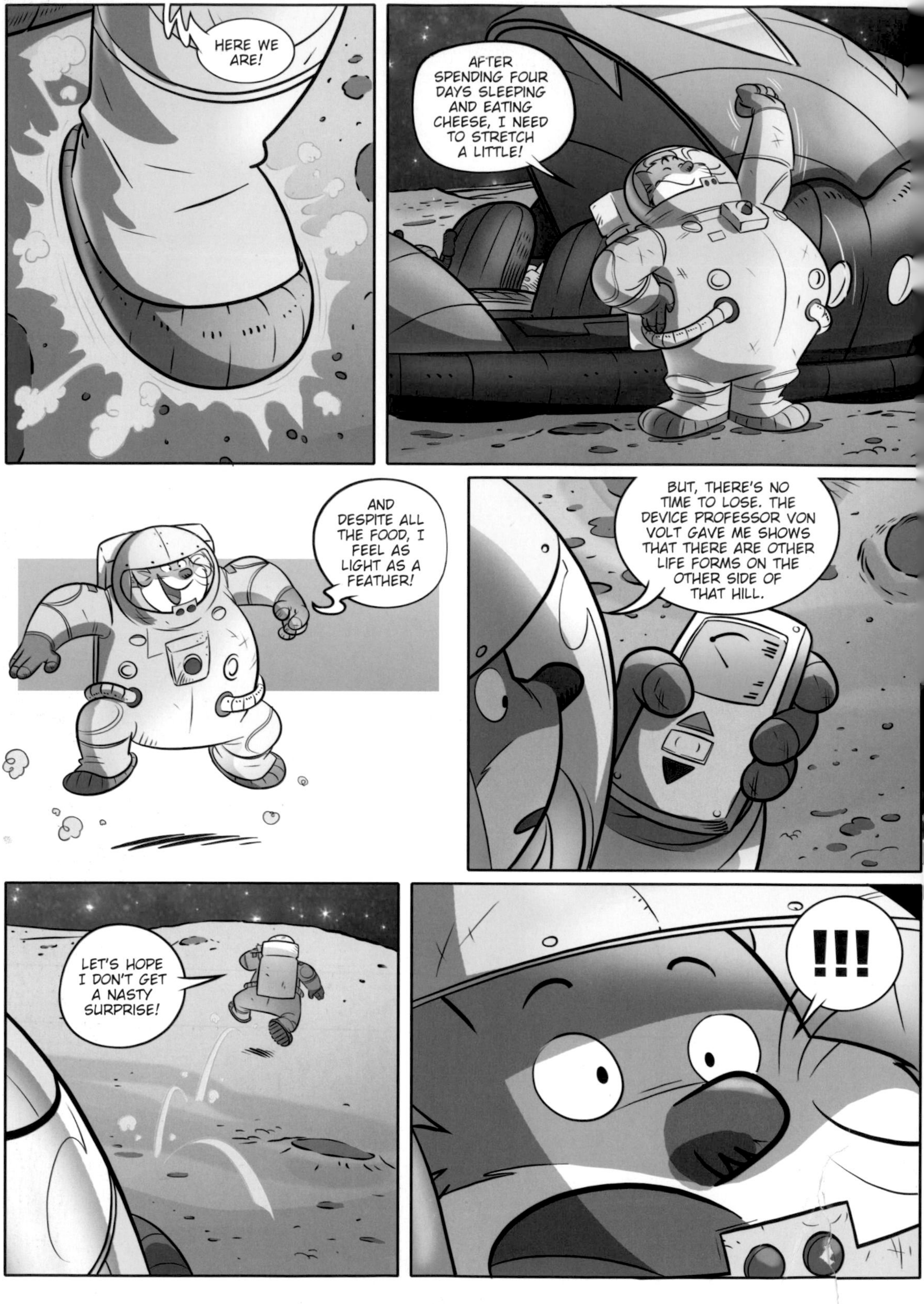
HERE WE ARE!
AFTER SPENDING FOUR DAYS SLEEPING AND EATING CHEESE, I NEED TO STRETCH A LITTLE!
AND DESPITE ALL THE FOOD, I FEEL AS LIGHT AS A FEATHER!
BUT, THERE'S NO TIME TO LOSE. THE DEVICE PROFESSOR VON VOLT GAVE ME SHOWS THAT THERE ARE OTHER LIFE FORMS ON THE OTHER SIDE OF THAT HILL.
LET'S HOPE I DON'T GET A NASTY SURPRISE!
!!!

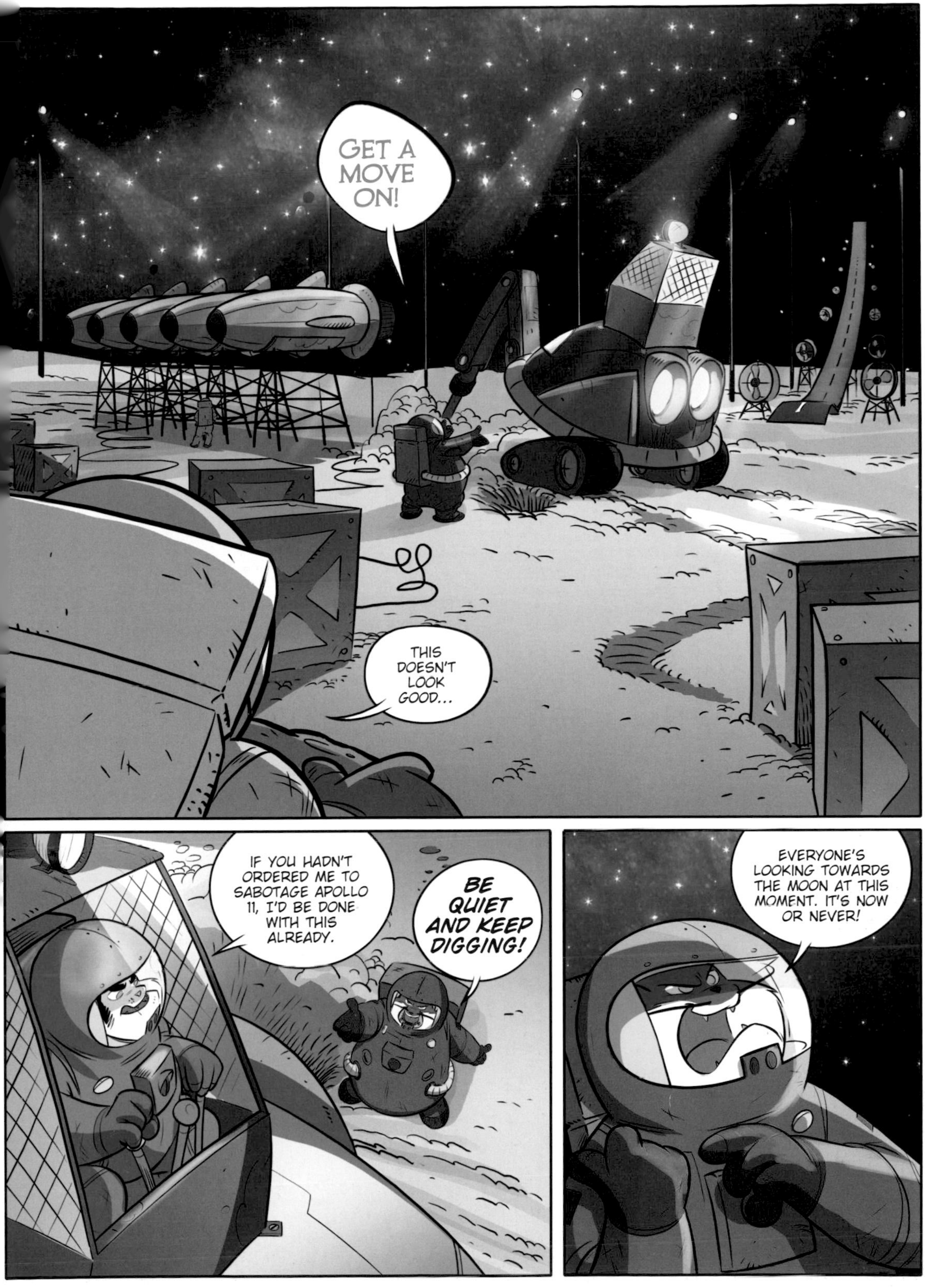
GET A MOVE ON!
THIS DOESN'T LOOK GOOD...
IF YOU HADN'T ORDERED ME TO SABOTAGE APOLLO 11, I'D BE DONE WITH THIS ALREADY.
BE QUIET AND KEEP DIGGING!
EVERYONE'S LOOKING TOWARDS THE MOON AT THIS MOMENT. IT'S NOW OR NEVER!

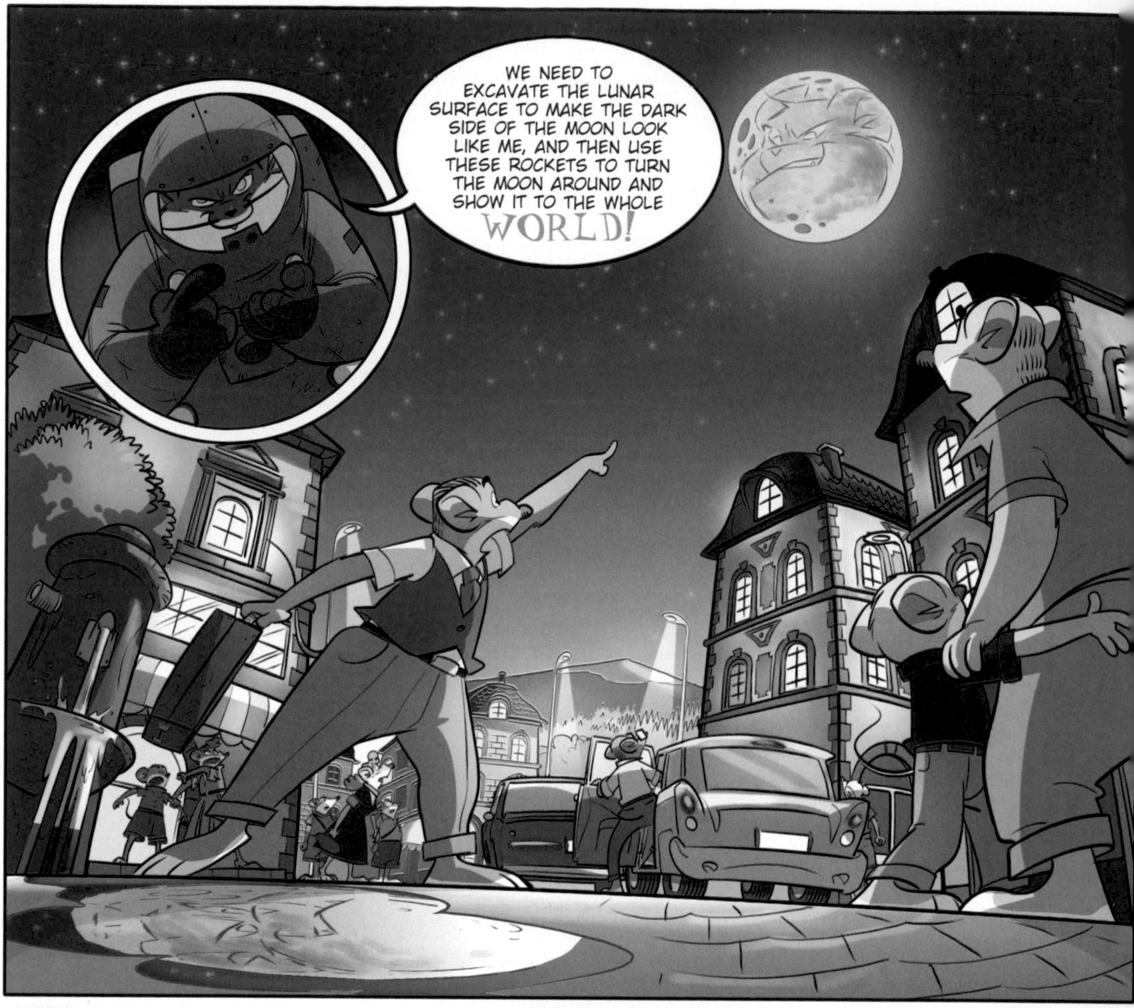
WE NEED TO EXCAVATE THE LUNAR SURFACE TO MAKE THE DARK SIDE OF THE MOON LOOK LIKE ME, AND THEN USE THESE ROCKETS TO TURN THE MOON AROUND AND SHOW IT TO THE WHOLE WORLD!

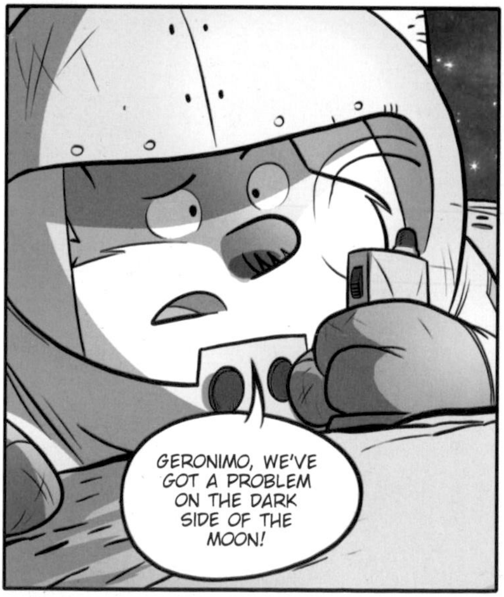
GERONIMO, WE'VE GOT A PROBLEM ON THE DARK SIDE OF THE MOON!

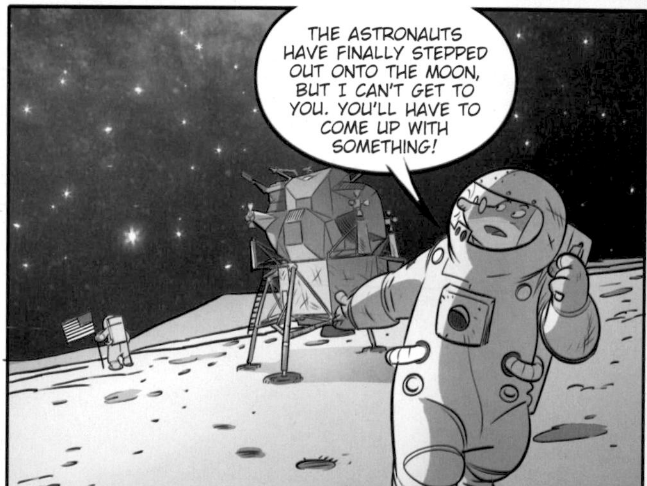
THE ASTRONAUTS HAVE FINALLY STEPPED OUT ONTO THE MOON, BUT I CAN'T GET TO YOU. YOU'LL HAVE TO COME UP WITH SOMETHING!

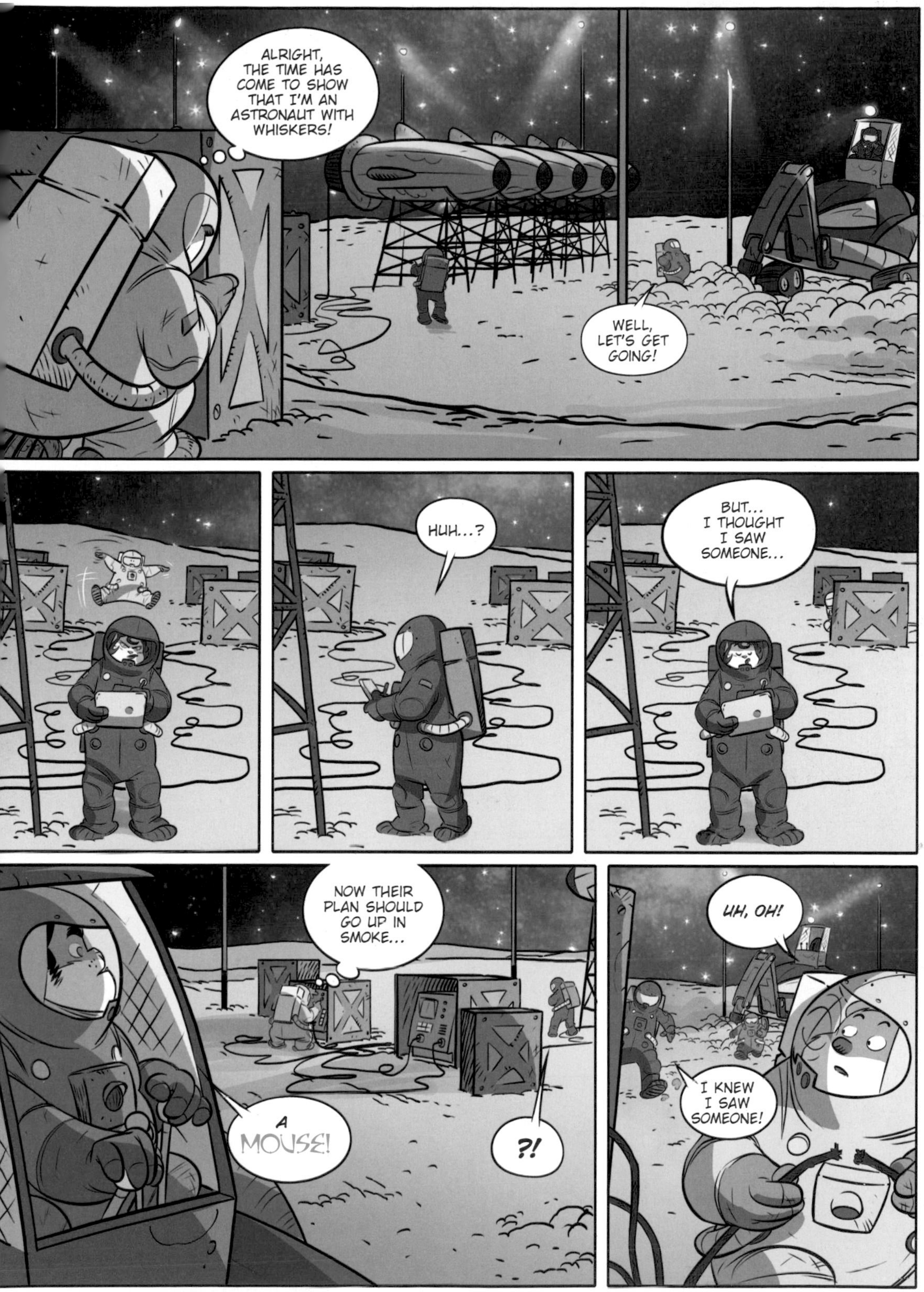
ALRIGHT, THE TIME HAS COME TO SHOW THAT I'M AN ASTRONAUT WITH WHISKERS!
WELL, LET'S GET GOING!
HUH...?
BUT... I THOUGHT I SAW SOMEONE...
NOW THEIR PLAN SHOULD GO UP IN SMOKE...
A MOUSE!
?!
UH, OH!
I KNEW I SAW SOMEONE!

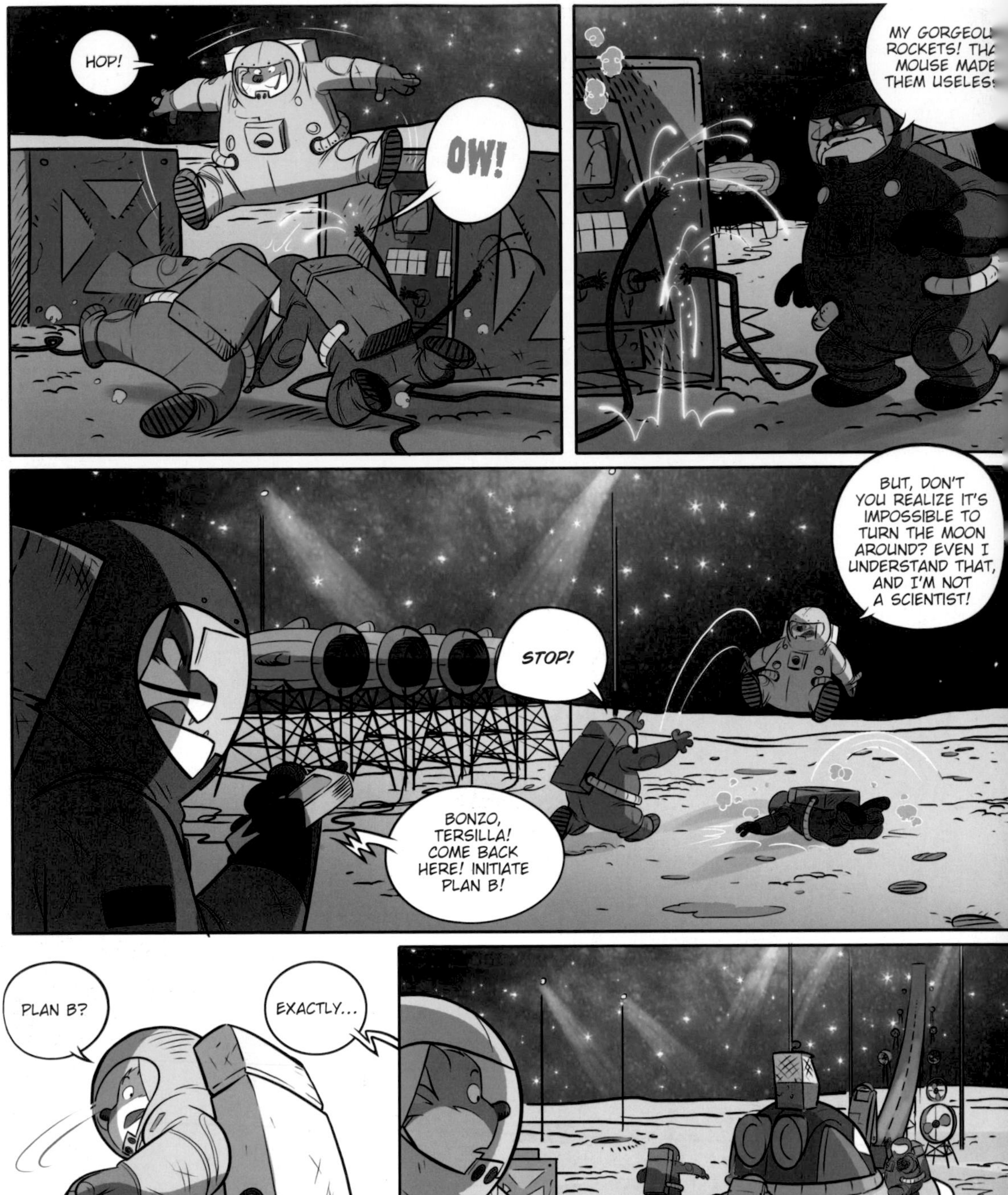
HOP!
OW!
MY GORGEOU ROCKETS! THA MOUSE MADE THEM USELES
BUT, DON'T YOU REALIZE IT'S IMPOSSIBLE TO TURN THE MOON AROUND? EVEN I UNDERSTAND THAT, AND I'M NOT A SCIENTIST!
STOP!
BONZO, TERSILLA! COME BACK HERE! INITIATE PLAN B!
PLAN B?
EXACTLY...
THIS COMPLEX SYSTEM OF FANS WILL PROPEL THE CATJET FAR INTO SPACE, AND TURN THE MOON TOO! YOU'LL NEVER CATCH US IN TIME!

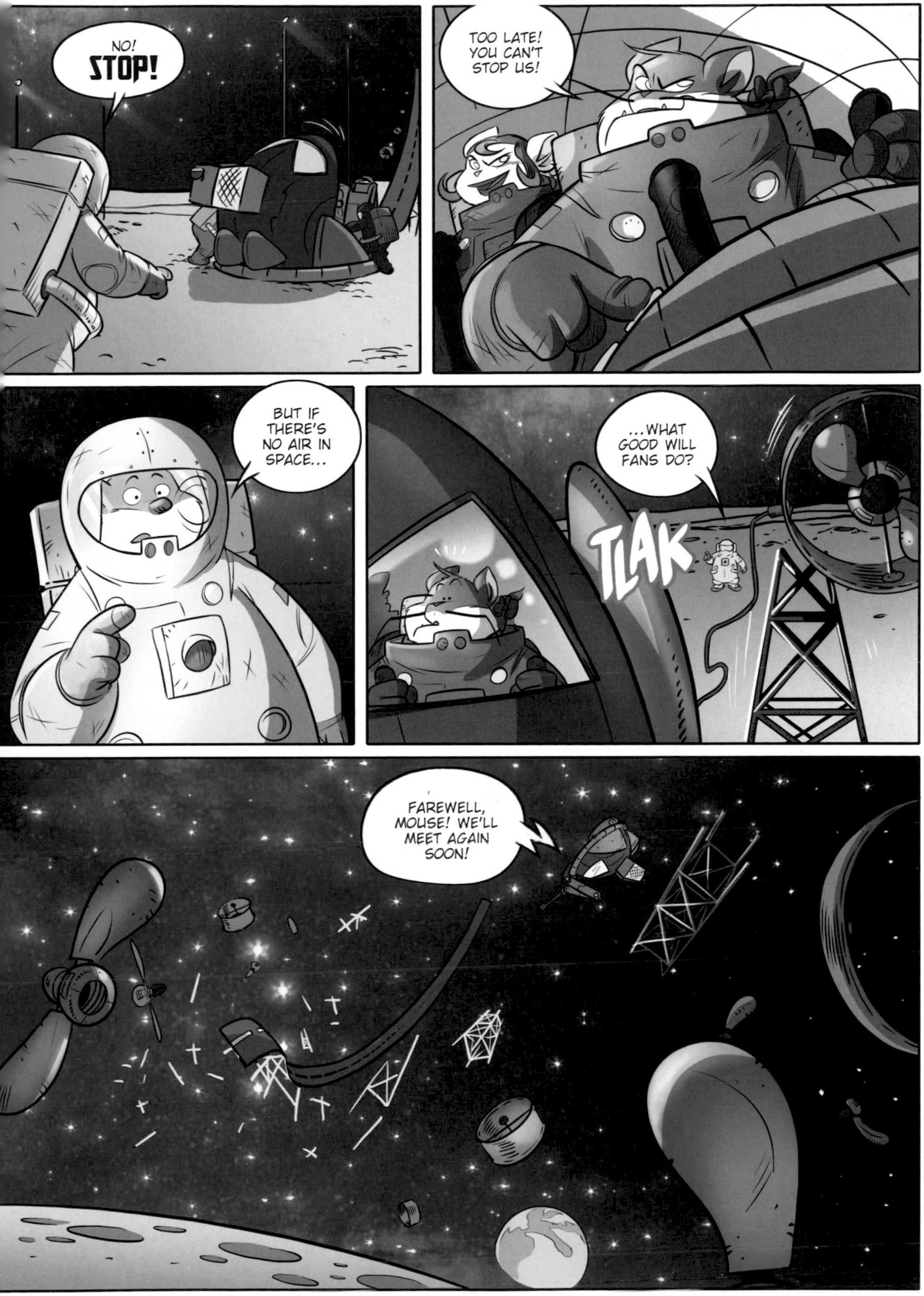
NO! STOP!
TOO LATE! YOU CAN'T STOP US!
BUT IF THERE'S NO AIR IN SPACE...
...WHAT GOOD WILL FANS DO?
TLAK
FAREWELL, MOUSE! WE'LL MEET AGAIN SOON!

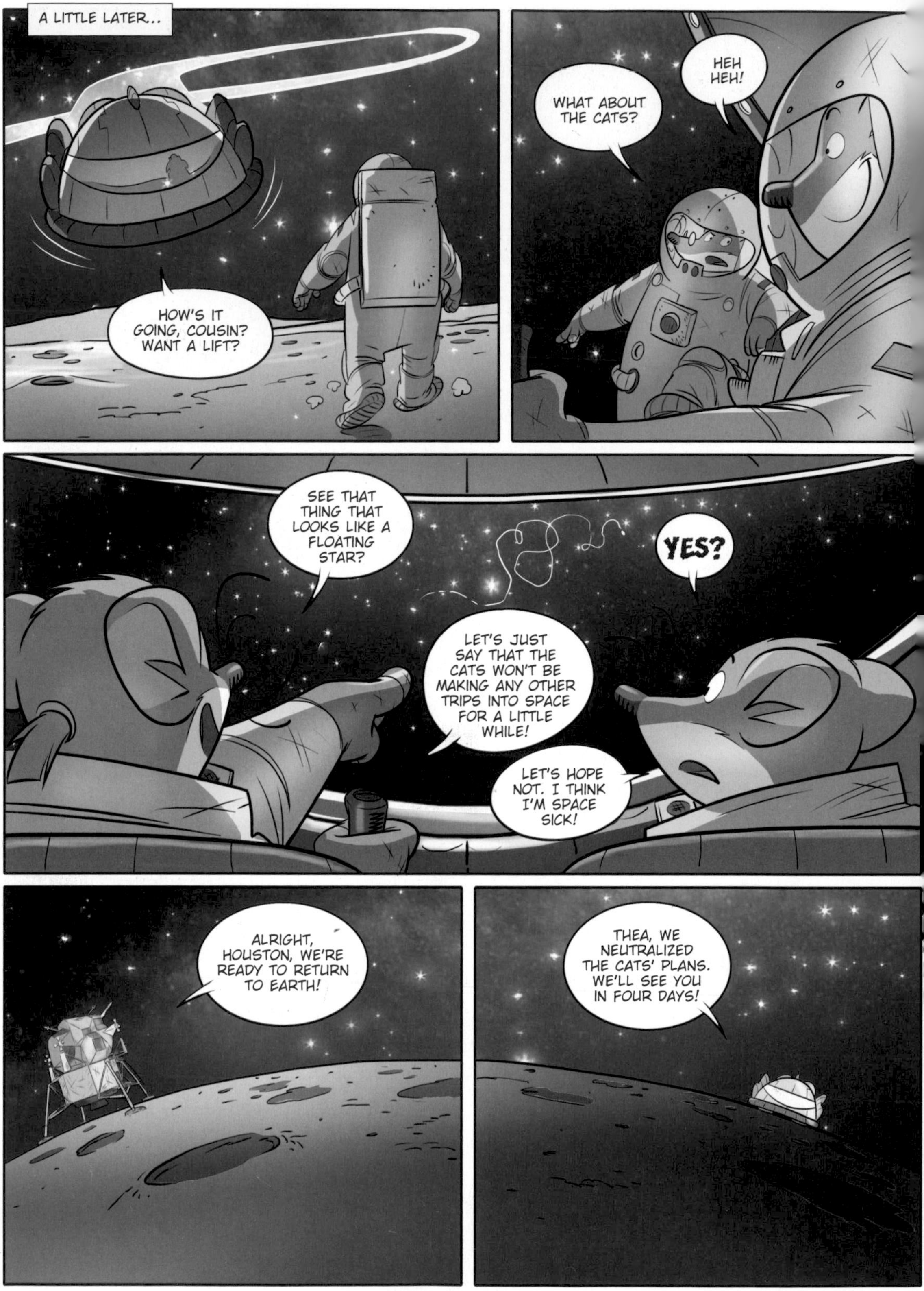

A LITTLE LATER...
HOW'S IT GOING, COUSIN? WANT A LIFT?
WHAT ABOUT THE CATS?
HEH HEH!
SEE THAT THING THAT LOOKS LIKE A FLOATING STAR?
YES?
LET'S JUST SAY THAT THE CATS WON'T BE MAKING ANY OTHER TRIPS INTO SPACE FOR A LITTLE WHILE!
LET'S HOPE NOT. I THINK I'M SPACE SICK!
ALRIGHT, HOUSTON, WE'RE READY TO RETURN TO EARTH!
THEA, WE NEUTRALIZED THE CATS' PLANS. WE'LL SEE YOU IN FOUR DAYS!

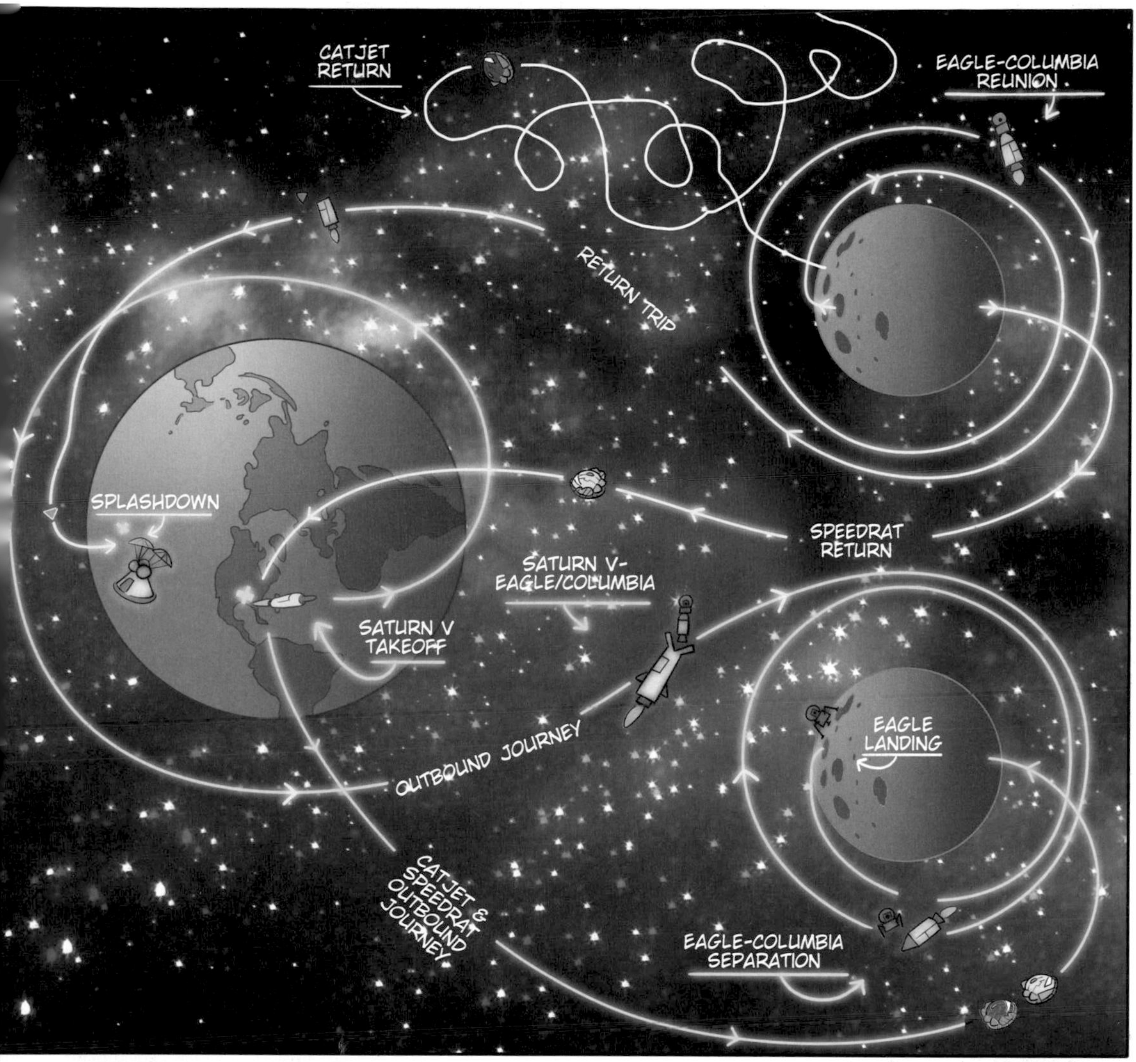
CATJET RETURN
EAGLE-COLUMBIA REUNION
RETURN TRIP
SPLASHDOWN
SPEEDRAT RETURN
SATURN V-EAGLE/COLUMBIA
SATURN V TAKEOFF
OUTBOUND JOURNEY
EAGLE LANDING
CATJET & SPEEDRAT OUTBOUND JOURNEY
EAGLE-COLUMBIA SEPARATION

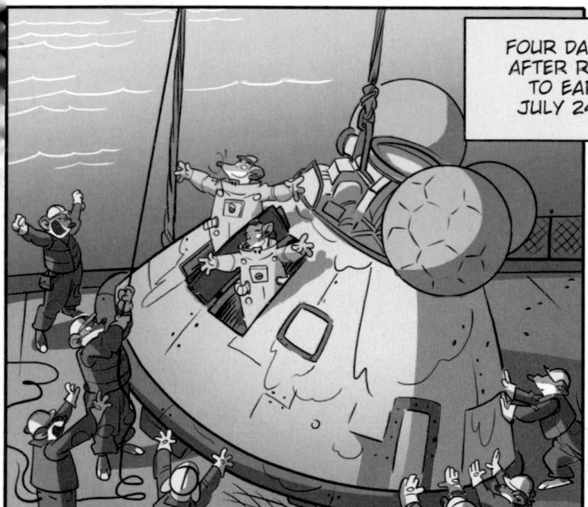
FOUR DAYS LATER, AFTER RETURNING TO EARTH, ON JULY 24, 1969...

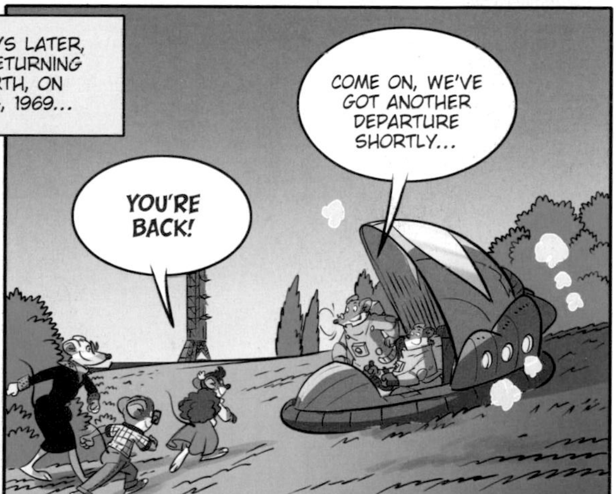
YOU'RE BACK!
COME ON, WE'VE GOT ANOTHER DEPARTURE SHORTLY...

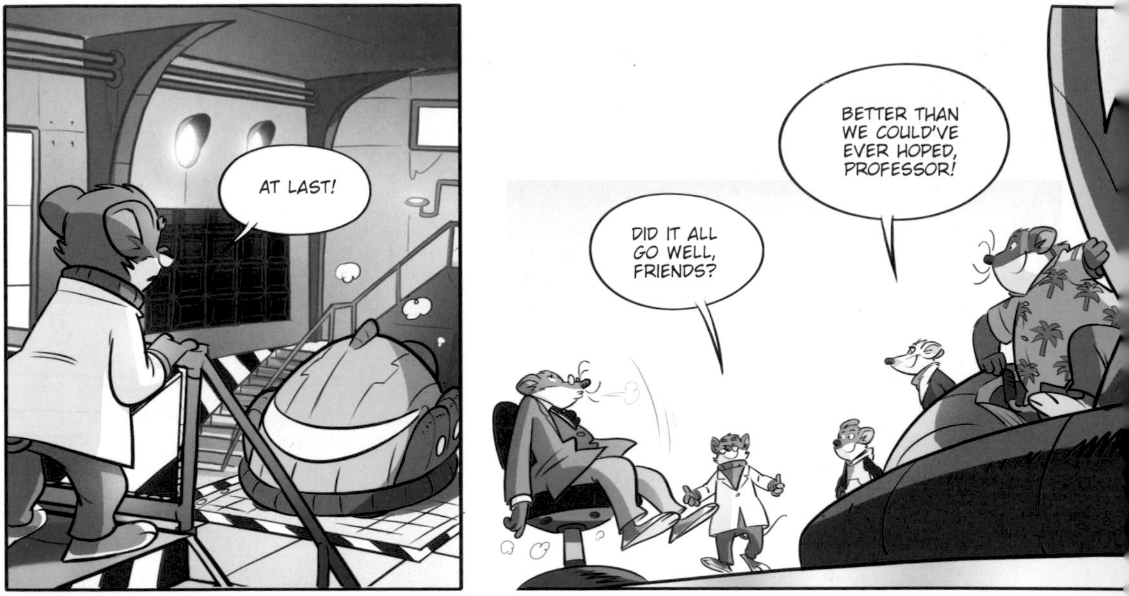
AT LAST!
DID IT ALL GO WELL, FRIENDS?
BETTER THAN WE COULD'VE EVER HOPED, PROFESSOR!

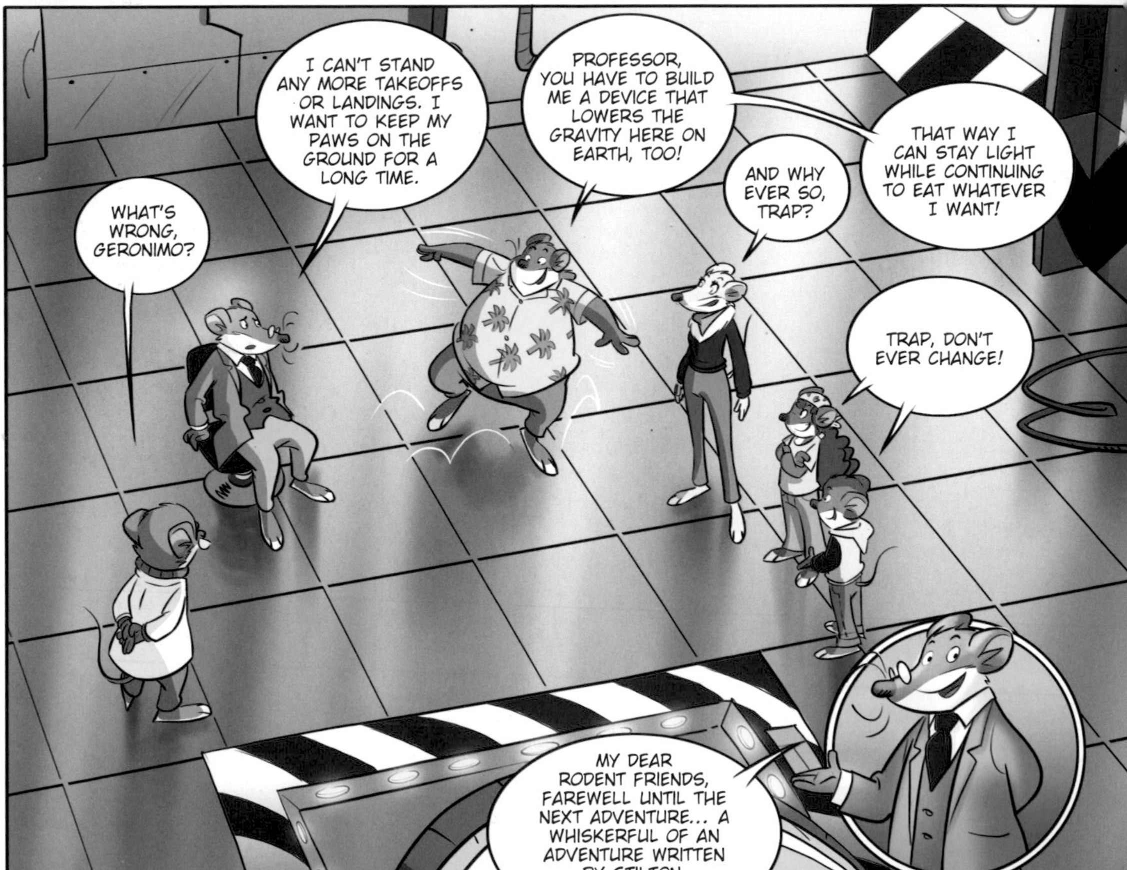
WHAT'S WRONG, GERONIMO?
I CAN'T STAND ANY MORE TAKEOFFS OR LANDINGS. I WANT TO KEEP MY PAWS ON THE GROUND FOR A LONG TIME.
PROFESSOR, YOU HAVE TO BUILD ME A DEVICE THAT LOWERS THE GRAVITY HERE ON EARTH, TOO!
AND WHY EVER SO, TRAP?
THAT WAY I CAN STAY LIGHT WHILE CONTINUING TO EAT WHATEVER I WANT!
TRAP, DON'T EVER CHANGE!
MY DEAR RODENT FRIENDS, FAREWELL UNTIL THE NEXT ADVENTURE... A WHISKERFUL OF AN ADVENTURE WRITTEN BY STILTON, Geronimo Stilton!

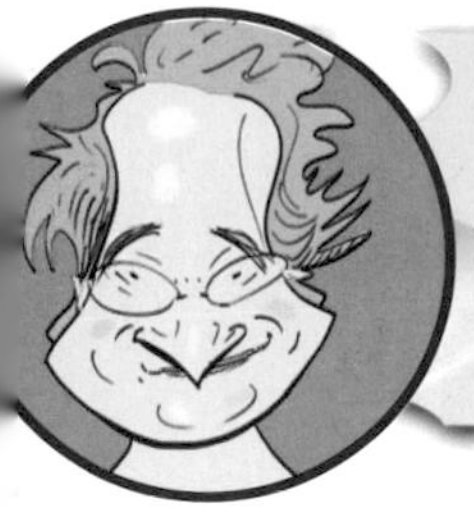

Watch Out For PAPERCUTZ

Welcome to the far-out, fourteenth GERONIMO STILTON graphic novel from Papercutz, those gravity-bound folks dedicated to publishing great graphic novels for all ages. I'm Salicrup, *Jim Salicrup*, the Editor-in-Chief at Ground Control. And this is also the first GERONIMO STILTON graphic novel in which Geronimo travels back to a time when I was actually alive! I may have only been 12-years old, but I was back there, when on July 21, 1969, Neil Armstrong became the first human to set foot on the surface of the moon.

I was recently reminded while watching *The Wind Rises*, the wonderful animated film by Hayao Miyazaki, what a tremendous impact aviation had on my father's generation— "The Greatest Generation," as named by journalist Tom Brokaw. My dad, when he was young, dreamed of being a pilot (he never fulfilled that dream unfortunately). For my generation, "The Baby Boomers," we were captivated by Space— "The Final Frontier." It was everywhere, when I was a kid! A couple of my favorite toys were a tiny model of the Apollo 11 Lunar Module and the Fireball XL5 rocket ship. On TV I loved watching shows such as *Star Trek* and *Lost in Space*. Even non-space shows seemed to have astronauts pop up in them—I remember an episode of *Gilligan's Island* that featured two Russian cosmonauts landing on their island by mistake. And on I Dream of Jeanie, the show was about an astronaut who stumbled upon a magical genie while walking along the beach. Just check out any cable network that runs these old TV shows or YouTube and you'll see plenty of such shows featuring astronauts.

As for comics, astronauts were all over the place! Just look at the start of "The Marvel Age of Comics"—*The Fantastic Four* was about four humans determined to beat the Russians into space. Of course things got complicated when they flew into a "Cosmic Storm" which wound up giving them super-powers, but that's a whole 'nother story! In the pages of *The Amazing Spider-Man #1*, Spidey rescues the son of his constant critic, J. Jonah Jameson, who just happens to be—you guessed it! – an astronaut! But Spidey's luck was such that the astronaut was still considered a real hero, while Spidey was treated like either a threat or menace to society. BENNY BREAKIRON #3 "The Twelve Trials of Benny Breakiron," which stars the super-strong French boy created by Peyo, the creator of THE SMURFS, features the following short gag…

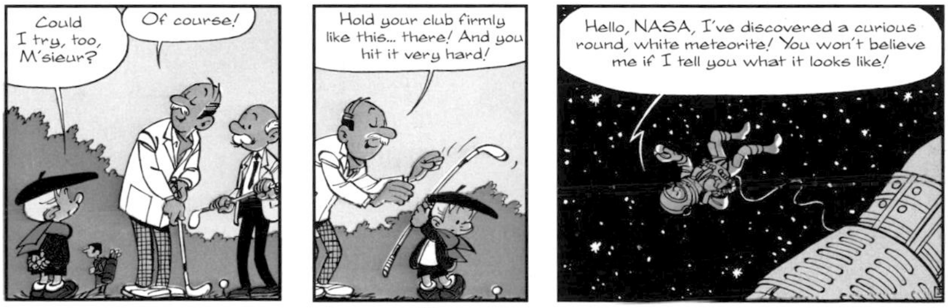

Could I try, too, M'sieur?
Of course!
Hold your club firmly like this... there! And you hit it very hard!
Hello, NASA, I've discovered a curious round, white meteorite! You won't believe me if I tell you what it looks like!

All I'm attempting to demonstrate is what a huge global impact the race to space had in the early 60s, permeating just about every aspect of pop culture. Almost every detail of "The First Mouse on the Moon" has countless precedents—*The Fantastic Four* did make it to the moon many times, and were even there when Neil Armstrong landed. The satirical super-hero the Tick's arch enemy Chairface Chippendale even tried to write his name on the moon—and even succeeded in getting the first $2^{1}/_{2}$ gigantic letters carved on the lunar surface. I could go on, but I suspect you can probably think of more examples yourself!

We hope you love "The First Mouse on the Moon," and hope you'll be back for GERONIMO STILTON #15 "All for Stilton, Stilton for All!" Think you can guess what *that* will be about?

See you in the future!

Jim

STAY IN TOUCH!

EMAIL:	salicrup@papercutz.com
WEB:	papercutz.com
TWITTER:	@papercutzgn
FACEBOOK:	PAPERCUTZGRAPHICNOVELS
FAN MAIL:	Papercutz, 160 Broadway, Suite 700, East Wing, New York, NY 10038

Caricature of Jim by Steve Brodner drawn at the MoCCA Art Fest.

Special preview of THEA STILTON #4 "Catching the Giant Wave!"

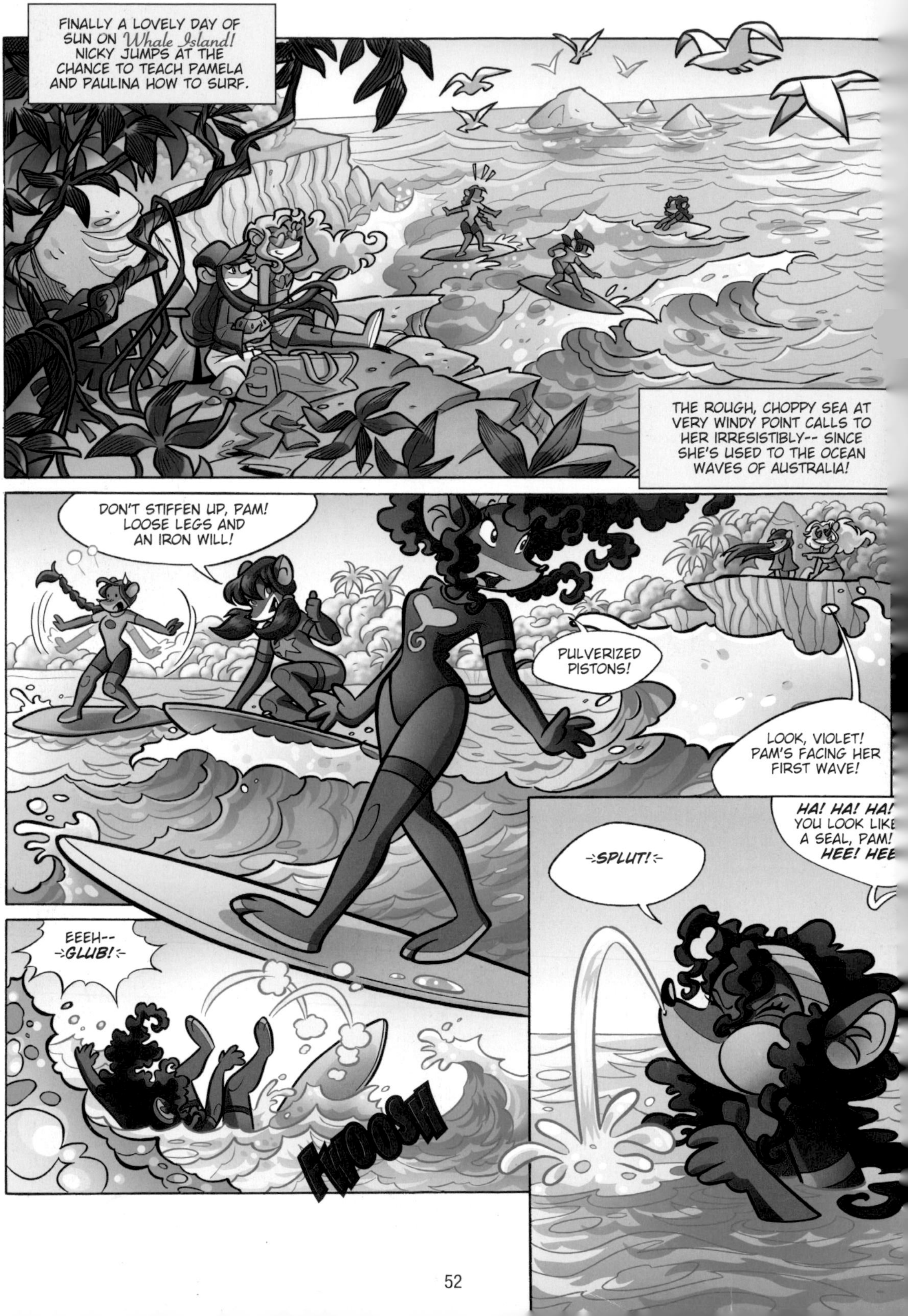

FINALLY A LOVELY DAY OF SUN ON Whale Island! NICKY JUMPS AT THE CHANCE TO TEACH PAMELA AND PAULINA HOW TO SURF.
THE ROUGH, CHOPPY SEA AT VERY WINDY POINT CALLS TO HER IRRESISTIBLY-- SINCE SHE'S USED TO THE OCEAN WAVES OF AUSTRALIA!
DON'T STIFFEN UP, PAM! LOOSE LEGS AND AN IRON WILL!
PULVERIZED PISTONS!
LOOK, VIOLET! PAM'S FACING HER FIRST WAVE!
EEEH-- -GLUB!-
FWOOSH
-SPLUT!-
HA! HA! HA! YOU LOOK LIKE A SEAL, PAM! HEE! HEE

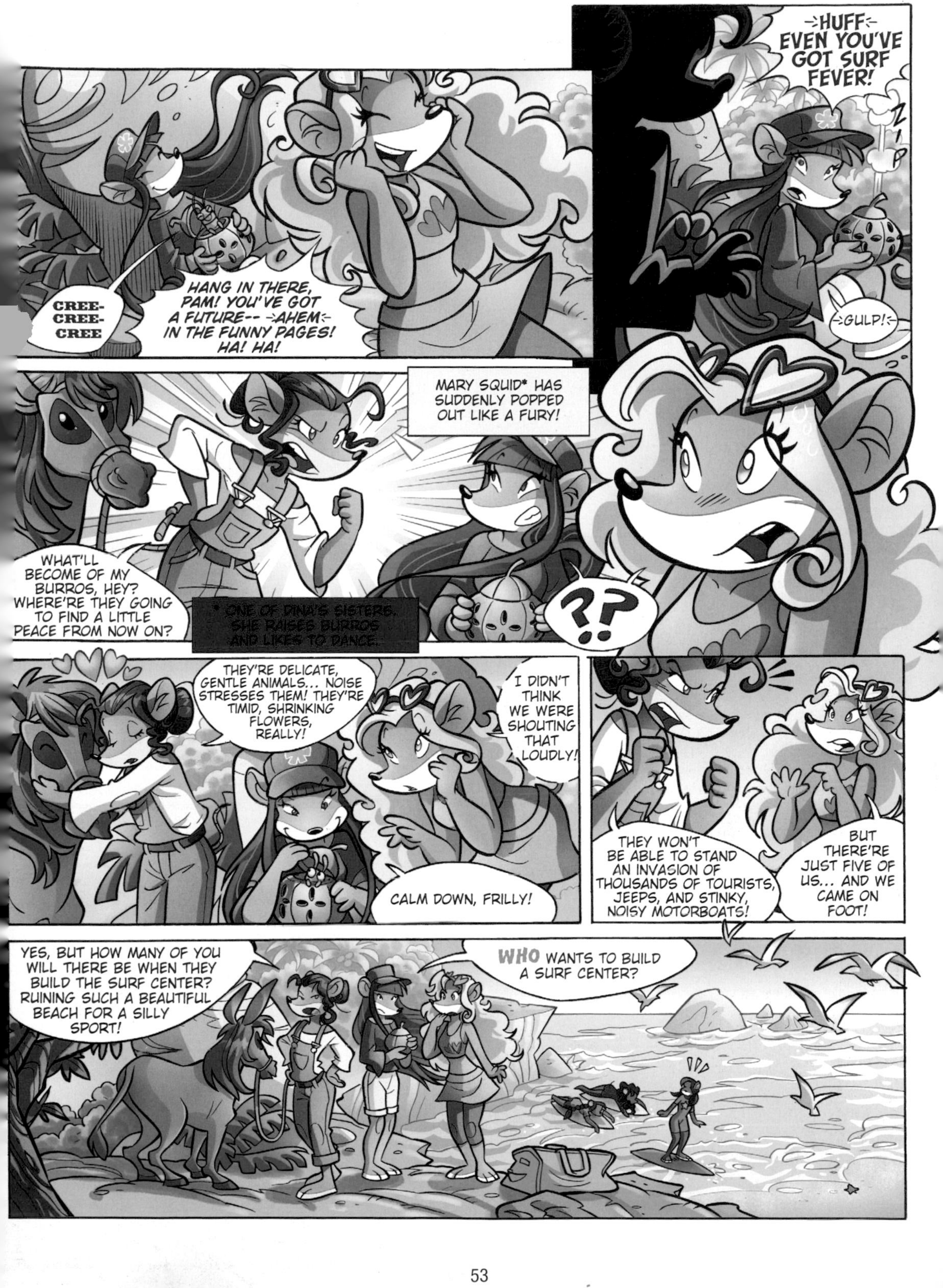
CREE-
CREE-
CREE
HANG IN THERE, PAM! YOU'VE GOT A FUTURE-- -AHEM- IN THE FUNNY PAGES! HA! HA!
-HUFF- EVEN YOU'VE GOT SURF FEVER!
ZIP
-GULP!-
MARY SQUID* HAS SUDDENLY POPPED OUT LIKE A FURY!
WHAT'LL BECOME OF MY BURROS, HEY? WHERE'RE THEY GOING TO FIND A LITTLE PEACE FROM NOW ON?
* ONE OF DINA'S SISTERS. SHE RAISES BURROS AND LIKES TO DANCE.
??
THEY'RE DELICATE, GENTLE ANIMALS... NOISE STRESSES THEM! THEY'RE TIMID, SHRINKING FLOWERS, REALLY!
I DIDN'T THINK WE WERE SHOUTING THAT LOUDLY!
CALM DOWN, FRILLY!
THEY WON'T BE ABLE TO STAND AN INVASION OF THOUSANDS OF TOURISTS, JEEPS, AND STINKY, NOISY MOTORBOATS!
BUT THERE'RE JUST FIVE OF US... AND WE CAME ON FOOT!
YES, BUT HOW MANY OF YOU WILL THERE BE WHEN THEY BUILD THE SURF CENTER? RUINING SUCH A BEAUTIFUL BEACH FOR A SILLY SPORT!
WHO WANTS TO BUILD A SURF CENTER?

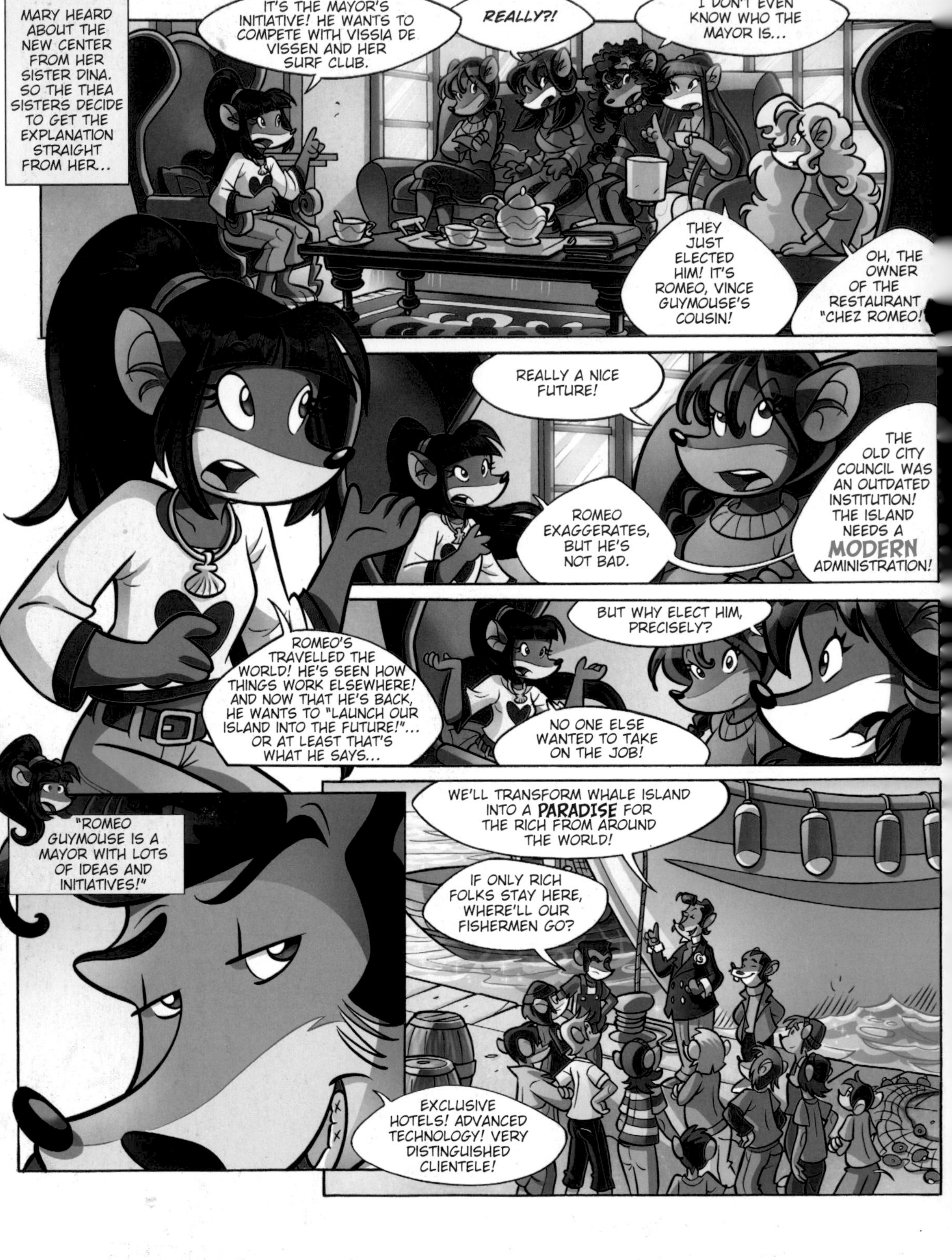
MARY HEARD ABOUT THE NEW CENTER FROM HER SISTER DINA. SO THE THEA SISTERS DECIDE TO GET THE EXPLANATION STRAIGHT FROM HER..
IT'S THE MAYOR'S INITIATIVE! HE WANTS TO COMPETE WITH VISSIA DE VISSEN AND HER SURF CLUB.
REALLY?!
I DON'T EVEN KNOW WHO THE MAYOR IS...
THEY JUST ELECTED HIM! IT'S ROMEO, VINCE GUYMOUSE'S COUSIN!
OH, THE OWNER OF THE RESTAURANT "CHEZ ROMEO!"
REALLY A NICE FUTURE!
THE OLD CITY COUNCIL WAS AN OUTDATED INSTITUTION! THE ISLAND NEEDS A MODERN ADMINISTRATION!
ROMEO EXAGGERATES, BUT HE'S NOT BAD.
BUT WHY ELECT HIM, PRECISELY?
ROMEO'S TRAVELLED THE WORLD! HE'S SEEN HOW THINGS WORK ELSEWHERE! AND NOW THAT HE'S BACK, HE WANTS TO "LAUNCH OUR ISLAND INTO THE FUTURE!"... OR AT LEAST THAT'S WHAT HE SAYS...
NO ONE ELSE WANTED TO TAKE ON THE JOB!
"ROMEO GUYMOUSE IS A MAYOR WITH LOTS OF IDEAS AND INITIATIVES!"
WE'LL TRANSFORM WHALE ISLAND INTO A PARADISE FOR THE RICH FROM AROUND THE WORLD!
IF ONLY RICH FOLKS STAY HERE, WHERE'LL OUR FISHERMEN GO?
EXCLUSIVE HOTELS! ADVANCED TECHNOLOGY! VERY DISTINGUISHED CLIENTELE!

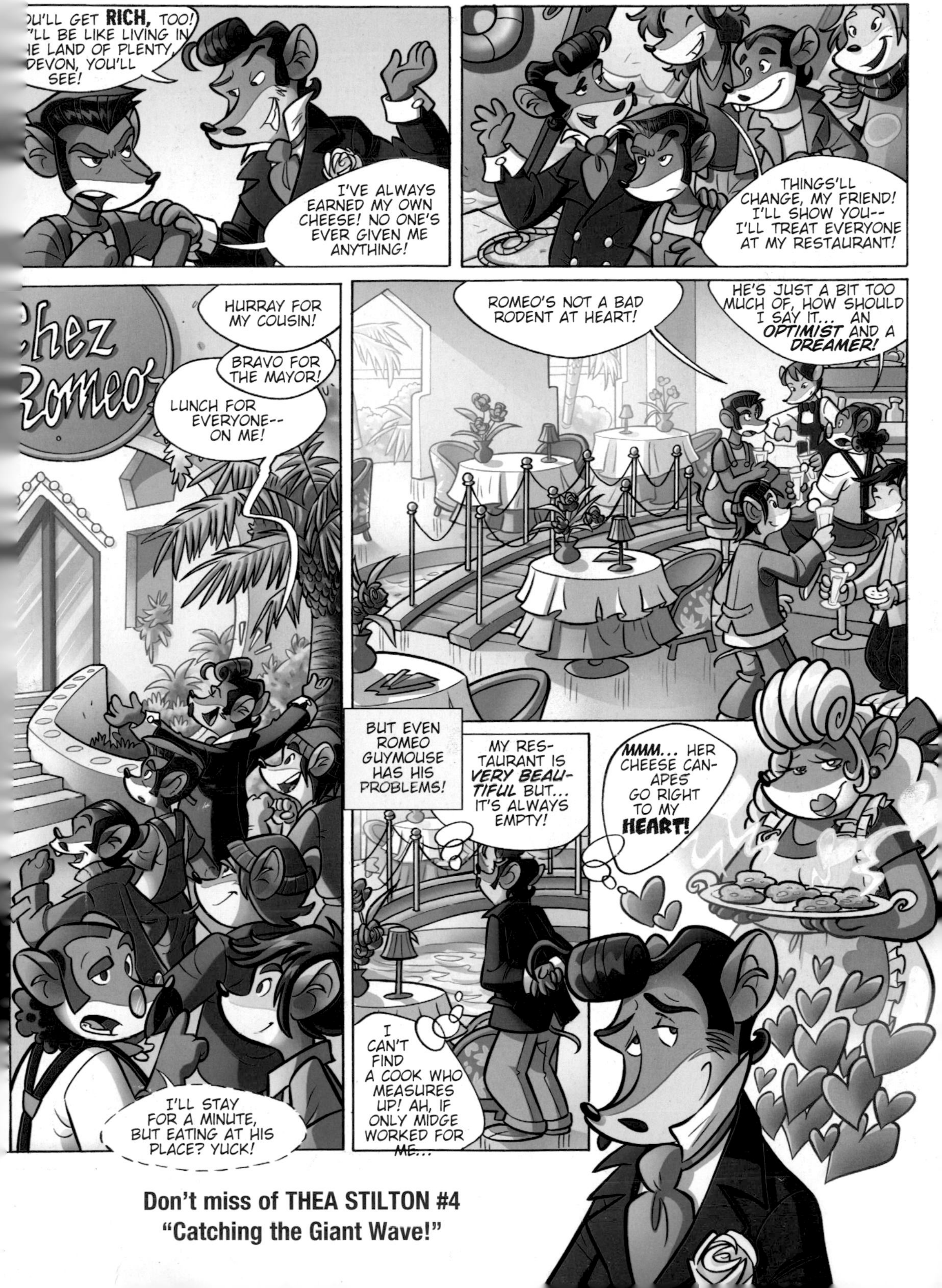

OU'LL GET RICH, TOO! 'LL BE LIKE LIVING IN HE LAND OF PLENTY, DEVON, YOU'LL SEE!
I'VE ALWAYS EARNED MY OWN CHEESE! NO ONE'S EVER GIVEN ME ANYTHING!
THINGS'LL CHANGE, MY FRIEND! I'LL SHOW YOU-- I'LL TREAT EVERYONE AT MY RESTAURANT!
Chez Romeo
HURRAY FOR MY COUSIN!
BRAVO FOR THE MAYOR!
LUNCH FOR EVERYONE-- ON ME!
I'LL STAY FOR A MINUTE, BUT EATING AT HIS PLACE? YUCK!
ROMEO'S NOT A BAD RODENT AT HEART!
HE'S JUST A BIT TOO MUCH OF, HOW SHOULD I SAY IT... AN OPTIMIST AND A DREAMER!
BUT EVEN ROMEO GUYMOUSE HAS HIS PROBLEMS!
MY RESTAURANT IS VERY BEAUTIFUL BUT... IT'S ALWAYS EMPTY!
I CAN'T FIND A COOK WHO MEASURES UP! AH, IF ONLY MIDGE WORKED FOR ME...
MMM... HER CHEESE CANAPES GO RIGHT TO MY HEART!

Don't miss of THEA STILTON #4
"Catching the Giant Wave!"

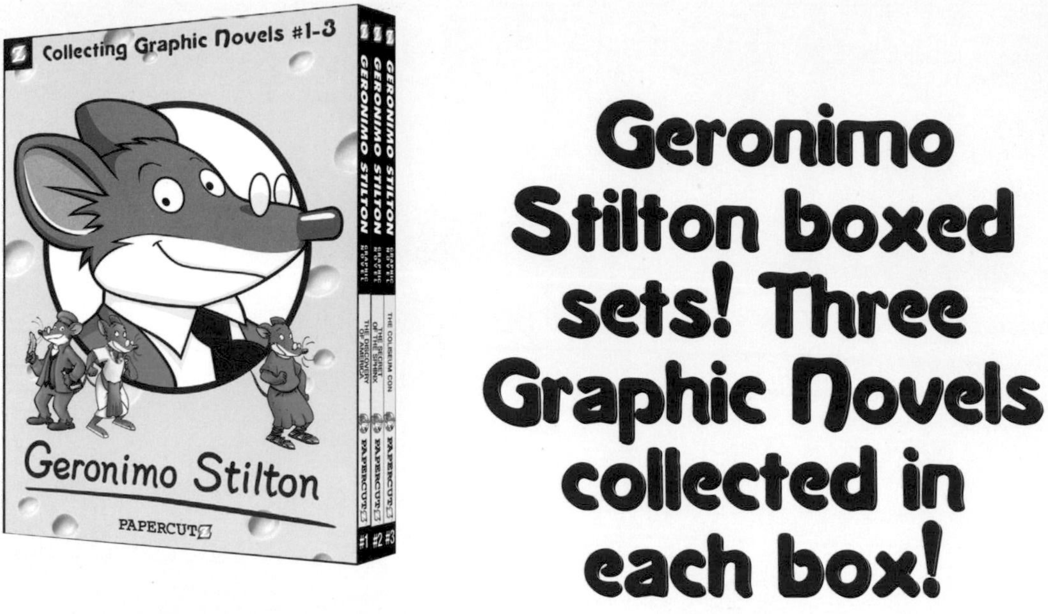
Collecting Graphic Novels #1-3
GERONIMO STILTON
GERONIMO STILTON
GERONIMO STILTON
THE COLISEUM CON
THE DISCOVERY OF AMERICA
Geronimo Stilton
PAPERCUTZ
#1 #2 #3

Geronimo Stilton boxed sets! Three Graphic Novels collected in each box!

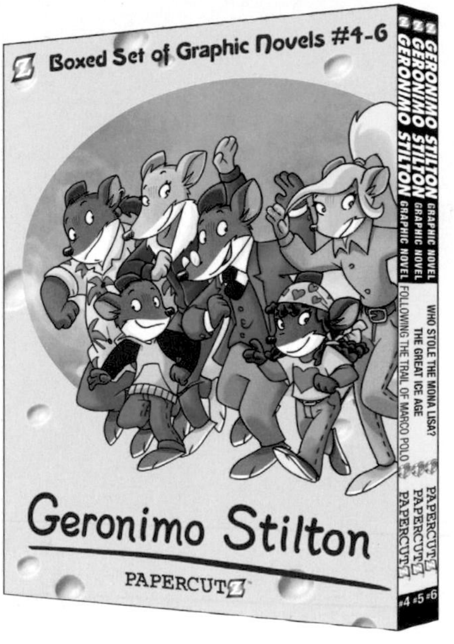
Boxed Set of Graphic Novels #4-6
GERONIMO STILTON GRAPHIC NOVEL
GERONIMO STILTON GRAPHIC NOVEL
GERONIMO STILTON GRAPHIC NOVEL
WHO STOLE THE MONA LISA?
THE GREAT ICE AGE
FOLLOWING THE TRAIL OF MARCO POLO
Geronimo Stilton
PAPERCUTZ
#4 #5 #6

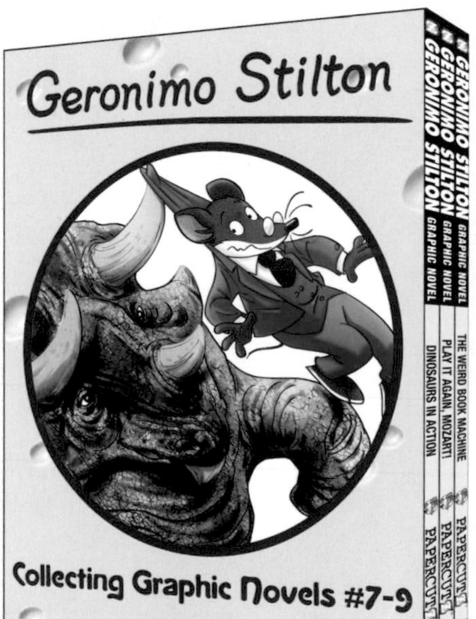
Geronimo Stilton
GERONIMO STILTON GRAPHIC NOVEL
GERONIMO STILTON GRAPHIC NOVEL
GERONIMO STILTON GRAPHIC NOVEL
THE WEIRD BOOK MACHINE
PLAY IT AGAIN, MOZART!
DINOSAURS IN ACTION
Collecting Graphic Novels #7-9
PAPERCUTZ
#7 #8 #9

Available at booksellers everywhere.

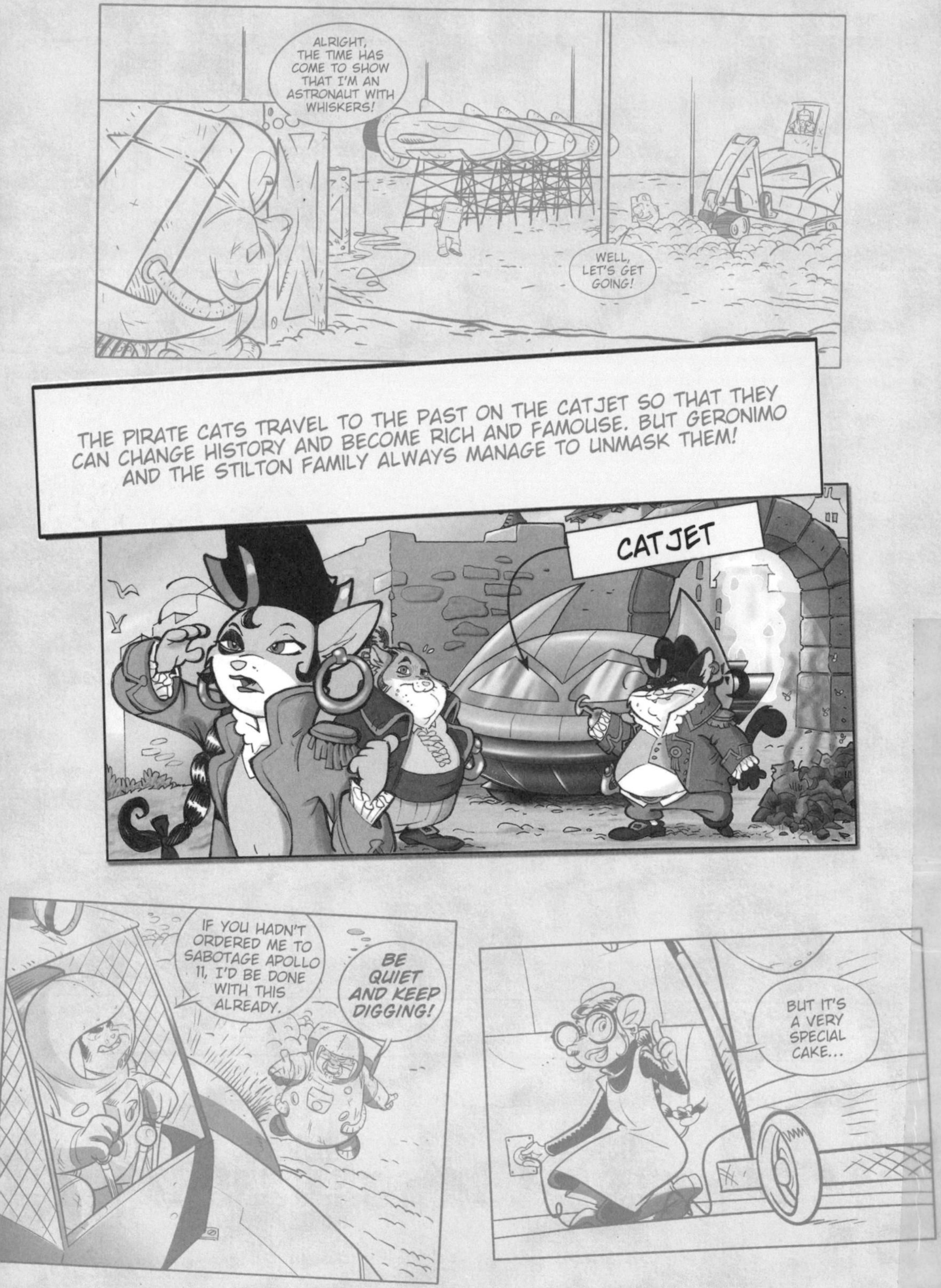

ALRIGHT, THE TIME HAS COME TO SHOW THAT I'M AN ASTRONAUT WITH WHISKERS!
WELL, LET'S GET GOING!
THE PIRATE CATS TRAVEL TO THE PAST ON THE CATJET SO THAT THEY CAN CHANGE HISTORY AND BECOME RICH AND FAMOUSE. BUT GERONIMO AND THE STILTON FAMILY ALWAYS MANAGE TO UNMASK THEM!
CATJET
IF YOU HADN'T ORDERED ME TO SABOTAGE APOLLO 11, I'D BE DONE WITH THIS ALREADY.
BE QUIET AND KEEP DIGGING!
BUT IT'S A VERY SPECIAL CAKE...